DEEP
SEA

ALSO BY ANNIKA THOR

A Faraway Island
WINNER OF THE MILDRED L. BATCHELDER AWARD
FOR AN OUTSTANDING CHILDREN'S BOOK
ORIGINALLY PUBLISHED IN A FOREIGN LANGUAGE

The Lily Pond
WINNER OF THE MILDRED L. BATCHELDER HONOR AWARD
FOR AN OUTSTANDING CHILDREN'S BOOK
ORIGINALLY PUBLISHED IN A FOREIGN LANGUAGE

DEEP SEA

ANNIKA THOR

Translated from the Swedish by Linda Schenck

DELACORTE PRESS

Translation copyright © 2015 by Linda Schenck
Jacket photograph copyright © by Laurence Winram/Trevillion Images
All rights reserved. Published in the United States by Delacorte Press, an imprint of Random House Children's Books, a division of Random House LLC, a Penguin Random House Company, New York. Originally published in Sweden as *Havets djup* by Bonnier Carlsen, Stockholm, in 1998. Copyright 1998 by Annika Thor. This English translation is published by arrangement with Bonnier Group Agency, Stockholm, Sweden.

Delacorte Press is a registered trademark and the colophon is a trademark of Random House LLC.

Visit us on the Web! randomhouseteens.com

Educators and librarians, for a variety of teaching tools, visit us at RHTeachersLibrarians.com

Library of Congress Cataloging-in-Publication Data
Thor, Annika.
Deep sea / Annika Thor ; translated from the Swedish by Linda Schenck. — First American edition.
pages cm
Companion book to: A faraway island and The Lily pond.
"Originally published in Sweden as *Havets djup* by Annika Thor, copyright 1998 by Annika Thor, by Bonnier Carlsen, Stockholm, in 1998."
Summary: Nearly four years after leaving Vienna to escape the Nazis, Stephie Steiner, now sixteen, and her sister Nellie, eleven, are still living in Sweden, worrying about their parents and striving to succeed in school, and at odds with each other despite their mutual love.
ISBN 978-0-385-74385-3 (hc) — ISBN 978-0-385-37134-6 (ebook) — ISBN 978-0-375-99132-5 (glb) 1. World War, 1939–1945—Refugees—Juvenile fiction. [1. World War, 1939–1945—Refugees—Fiction. 2. Refugees—Fiction. 3. Sisters—Fiction. 4. Schools—Fiction. 5. Friendship—Fiction. 6. Jews—Sweden—Fiction. 7. Göteborg (Sweden)—History—20th century—Fiction. 8. Sweden—History—Gustav V, 1907–1950—Fiction.]
I. Schenck, Linda, translator. II. Title.
PZ7.T3817Dee 2015
[Fic]—dc23
2014005586

Printed in the United States of America
10 9 8 7 6 5 4 3 2 1
First American Edition

DEEP
SEA

1

The tram rattles down the wide street. Stephie stares out the window without really seeing anything. The roads, houses, shops, and flower beds along the route to and from school have all become so familiar they're invisible to her. Somewhere at the back of her mind, other streets and houses loom. But they are mere shadows, the memory of a dream.

"A penny for your thoughts!"

Stephie's eyes shift from the window to her friend May, who is sitting next to her.

"None in particular," she says.

"It's lucky you don't have to ride alone," says May. "I think you'd forget to get off."

With a piercing squeal, the tram pulls in at Sandarna.

Stephie and May stand up, along with most of the remaining passengers who live far from the center of town. Their tram route meanders through the whole city and passes through Mayhill, where May's family used to live. Although Sandarna isn't the last stop, it's the last outpost of the city, before the area becomes more rural. Once it has finished climbing the slope and made its turn, the nearly empty tram will cross the city limit and continue toward the sea, passing the fancy summerhouses in Långedrag and running all the way to the bathhouse at Saltholmen.

Stephie lives at the edge of the city. All the way out, as far as you can get. Just like when she lived on the island, where she still has her second home, with Aunt Märta and Uncle Evert. The first time Stephie saw their house on the barren west side of the island, at the opposite tip from the sheltered harbor and little village, she thought she must be at the end of the world.

But when you have to live thousands of miles from your home and your parents, you always feel far away. It doesn't really matter where you are.

The tram stops, and the girls get off and cross the street. Straight ahead is a big white elementary school attended by hundreds of children from the neighborhood's many large families. Most of May's little sisters and brothers are students there. She also has two siblings who haven't even started school yet, as well as an older sister, Britten, closest to May in age, who had to quit after primary school last spring and take a job as an errand girl at the bakery. Almost all the children in the area quit school after the compulsory six years. May is an exception; her high grades got her a scholarship, which allowed her to continue her education at the girls' grammar school in town.

"I'm worried sick about our math test!" says May. "I'll never pass. I just know it. And if I fail this one, too, Miss Björk is going to have to flunk me. Then I'll never get into high school."

Stephie and May are in their third and final year of grammar school now. Next fall, they'll start high school if their grades are good enough to win them scholarships again. Everyone in the class is focused on grades, but Stephie and May are the only ones who won't be able to go on if they don't get scholarships.

"You'll get through," says Stephie. "I'll help."

&

In the city center, there are many stately apartment buildings with a dark labyrinth of courtyards at their rear, where a myriad of outbuildings and sheds are separated by tall wooden fences. But the homes are so tightly lined up along the streets that passersby can't see what lies behind them.

Here in Sandarna, there are no courtyards. The apartment buildings are dotted along a slope, now covered with last year's snow-burnt grass, which will soon turn green. The off-white buildings are set at angles that give every apartment, each with its own balcony, some sun. Narrow paths lead up to the doors. The carpet-beating racks sport cheerful rag rugs being aired, and the whole area swarms with children.

The girls stop at the grocery store, the Co-Op, where they buy dinner on credit. Almost all the customers have their purchases written up in the ledger. Aunt Märta wouldn't approve. One of her many rules in life is "Be in debt to no one."

Then the girls head to the school day care to pick up Erik and Ninni. Erik is a confident six-year-old who doesn't really want to be seen with his big sister and her friend. He runs right off to play with the big boys. But three-year-old Ninni gives both girls hugs and kisses, and wants to be carried up the stairs. May picks her up, but Ninni reaches out for Stephie, who takes her from May. Halfway up, Ninni wants to change back.

"Spoiled rotten," May mutters, lugging her little sister up the last two fights to the fourth floor.

Stephie laughs. "And who's to blame for spoiling her?" she asks.

"I know, I know!"

Gunnel, who's eight, comes running up the stairs after them, wanting to tell them about something that happened at school. She takes Stephie by the hand, chatting eagerly. Gunnel is constantly admiring Stephie's black hair, dark eyes, and slight accent. She even

4

tries to imitate the way Stephie speaks Swedish. She always wants to be holding Stephie's hand or sitting on her lap. Stephie is happy to let her.

But occasionally, as Gunnel sits on her lap and twirls a lock of Stephie's long hair, Stephie's conscience bothers her. She starts thinking about Nellie, her own younger sister who still lives on the island with her foster parents, Auntie Alma and Uncle Sigurd. Since Stephie left to attend grammar school in Göteborg, she sees Nellie only one weekend a month and on school vacations. Nellie is ten now, going on eleven, a big girl who doesn't want to sit on anyone's lap.

Long ago, when they left Vienna before the war, Stephie promised their parents that she would take care of Nellie.

Stephie isn't sure she has lived up to that promise.

2

Stephie unlocks the door with the key she and May share. Britten has one of her own, but the younger children aren't allowed home until May and Stephie return from school, or unless their mother finishes her housekeeping job and gets home first.

There's a yellowish card on the doormat inside. Stephie picks it up, knowing without even looking what it is.

Early last autumn, she stopped receiving letters from her parents in Vienna. For several months, neither Stephie nor Nellie heard anything from them. Stephie's anxiety tightened uncomfortably in her stomach day after day, week after week, month after month.

In the end, a card arrived, identical to the one she's

holding in her hand. It came from Theresienstadt, a camp in Czechoslovakia, not far from Prague. The Germans had gathered thousands of Jews there—men, women, and children from Vienna, Berlin, Hamburg, and Prague. Stephie and Nellie would be there now, too, if their parents hadn't sent them to Sweden while there was still time.

The cards from Theresienstadt are always identical. Blank cards, like postcards but without pictures. And with very little text. Stephie has counted the words. Excluding the date and signature, there are always exactly thirty. She thinks people in the camp probably aren't allowed to write more than thirty words. She imagines someone sitting and counting the words on thousands of those cards. No wonder it takes at least a month, sometimes even longer, for them to arrive.

On one of the first cards, Papa asked Stephie if she could try to send food. He didn't say what they needed, but Aunt Märta helped Stephie fill a box with canned goods, dried fruit, oatmeal, and dark bread that kept well. Now they prepare a package every time Stephie goes home to the island. Aunt Märta pays for half the food, and Stephie saves her pocket money to pay for the other half. She also has some savings from the job she had as a delivery girl for a florist in town during the holiday season. In the winter, Aunt Märta knitted socks, mittens, and scarves and put them in the boxes. And every now and then, May's mother, Aunt Tyra, gives her a can of evaporated milk or a box of raisins to add to the next box.

May, too, knows that the card is from Stephie's parents. Putting Ninni down, she takes the bag of groceries from Stephie.

"Go into the bedroom," she says. "I'll take care of the kids and dinner."

As May heads for the kitchen with Ninni in tow, Gunnel stands in the hall, staring at Stephie, who is hanging up her coat.

"Gunnel!" May calls from the kitchen. "Come on in here and leave Stephie in peace."

Reluctantly, Gunnel moves toward the kitchen. Stephie takes the card with her into the bedroom she and May share with Britten and Gunnel. May's parents and Ninni sleep in the living room, while Kurre and Olle, who are eleven, share the kitchen settle. Erik sleeps in the bathroom, where there ought to be a bathtub, but the war has made delivery impossible. The landlord has promised them a tub as soon as the war ends.

Stephie sits down on her bed, one of the bottom bunks, and reads:

Theresienstadt, 13 March 1943

Darling!
Thank you for the box! Thanks and
regards to Aunt Märta. Your concern means

8

everything. Imagine! I'm singing "Queen of the Night" in The Magic Flute *camp opera!*

Kisses,
Mamma

Thirty words. Thirty words are so little. She can picture Mamma writing a draft in pencil, crossing things out, and making changes to be able to say all she wants to in that space. Maybe she changed *Dearest Stephie* to *Darling* just to save one word. Maybe she shortened the part about Aunt Märta from *Please thank Aunt Märta so much from us.* But she had been unable to resist that little exclamation, *Imagine!* And what did she mean, really? Was it possible to stage an opera in the camp? Could that be true?

Her mother's dream role had always been the Queen of the Night, but she never had the chance to sing it while she worked at the opera. She said she was too young for the role in those days. But before the Germans invaded, the family went to see a performance of *The Magic Flute.*

Well, maybe Theresienstadt isn't such an awful place after all, Stephie thinks. *If it's a place where you can put on a Mozart opera, it can't be all bad, can it?*

Stephie reads the little card over and over again, as if she might be able to extract something more from those thirty words. A whisper, a few notes of music, the answers to her questions.

A hubbub in the kitchen brings her back to reality. Ninni's hurt herself, and May is blaming Gunnel for not having kept a good enough eye on her little sister while May was cooking.

Stephie gets up off the bed. She tries to be as helpful as she possibly can with everything that needs to be done at May's. It's the least she can do. The relief committee does send some money to May's parents as a contribution to Stephie's room, board, and pocket money, but it's still not easy for them to have her living with them. Even without Stephie, there would be nine people in the apartment. Although it's larger than the family's old one on Kaptensgatan, it's still crowded.

When summer arrives, Stephie will return to the island as she did last summer, and Aunt Märta will get the money from the relief committee for those months. Whatever is left after food expenses and pocket money for Stephie will be deposited in a savings account at the post office bank in Stephie's name.

"For the future," says Aunt Märta.

The future. Stephie used to imagine an endless series of days. A road through an open landscape, not straight and easy, yet a road you could see and follow. Stephie can't see that road ahead of her anymore. She moves forward as if in a fog, one cautious step at a time.

Someday the fog will have to lift. Someday the war will have to end.

≈

Stephie goes into the kitchen. May has a pot of potatoes boiling on the stove, and she's frying herring. The scent of fish rises. Stephie sniffs. Since coming to Sweden, she has learned to like fish.

"Can I help you?" she asks.

"Is everything all right?" May counters.

"I think so."

"Well, would you set the table?"

Stephie takes out plates and glasses and knives and forks, putting them all on the kitchen table. It's a small kitchen; there's not enough room for all ten of them to eat at the same time. May and Stephie usually prepare dinner when they come home from school. When it's ready, they call in the younger children. Later, Aunt Tyra heats up what's left for Britten, May's father, and herself. Except on Sundays. On Sundays, they carry the kitchen table into the living room and they all eat together, some sitting at the main table, some around the low table in front of the couch.

The kitchen at Kaptensgatan was bigger, but otherwise everything is better here. It's a bright apartment, and in spite of not being so big, it feels light and airy. From the living room, you can look straight across the hall and out through the kitchen window. The wallpaper is nice and new, and there is linoleum on the floors. The kitchen has a gas stove and a china cupboard. There's hot running water in the kitchen and bathroom, as well as radiators under the windows, so the apartment stays warm. There's even a trash chute in the stairwell. When Aunt Tyra realized she no longer had to go outside to take out the garbage, tears came to her eyes.

"Just think," she said. "Regular people like us can live so well! Everything's so nice and new, and easy to take care of." She looked at her hands, red and chafed from all the housecleaning she does at home and for the wealthy families she works for. "Hot water in the apartment! Oh, how I would have loved that when all you kids were little. Think how much easier it would have been to keep you neat and clean! All but Erik, of course. He gets dirty the minute I turn my back!"

According to May, Sandarna is the start of a new era. An era in which workers will live in modern housing and exert influence in society. An era that will take root after the war.

After the war.

3

The last math test of the spring semester takes place in the school auditorium. Stephie's stomach tightens every time she enters this room to take a test. Rows of seats, a teacher on guard up front, and the acrid smell of test papers straight off the duplicating machine remind her of the German test in their first year, the time Miss Krantz falsely accused her of cheating. The memory lasts only for a flash; then the feeling passes.

Nowadays, she and Miss Krantz get along just fine. When Stephie's only explanation for why you say *der Mond* but *die Sonne* is that you can hear that it would be wrong otherwise, Miss Krantz just sighs and asks one of the other girls for the rule. She doesn't even criticize Stephie's Vienna dialect anymore but simply lets her speak her own way.

Stephie knows she has Miss Björk to thank for the improvement. She knows she gave Miss Krantz a talking-to, ordering her to treat Stephie better. It's amazing that she was able to get her German teacher to change her ways, since Miss Krantz has been teaching for thirty years, and Miss Björk only for five. Stephie feels very lucky to have a homeroom teacher like Miss Björk.

However, her geography teacher, Mr. Lundkvist, is still a problem. As recently as last autumn, he stood in front of the brand-new map of Europe, boasting about Germany's victories. He claimed that the new borders would be permanent, and that the German-occupied countries would eventually be integrated into the German Reich. He made a sweeping gesture along the whole of the map, from Norway in the north to Greece in the south, and from Paris in the west to Moscow in the east.

"And when that happens," Mr. Lundkvist went on, "Sweden won't be able to stay neutral. I'm sure you can see how that would be a geopolitical impossibility."

As usual, May objected, and, as usual, Mr. Lundkvist threatened to lower her grade.

But now it's spring 1943, and Mr. Lundkvist seems less sure of himself. Things aren't going so well for the Germans anymore. During the autumn, the English won a huge battle in the North African desert, and it looks as if the German army will soon have to withdraw entirely from North Africa. In the east, the Russians put a stop to the German offensive at one of the big Russian cities, Stalingrad. The Russians managed to surround the German troops and, in the end, defeated them. Stephie has seen newsreels of frozen, hollow-eyed soldiers surrendering, hands up.

"This is the beginning of the end," May's father said when they heard the news. "Soon the Thousand-Year Reich will fall. How could they have imagined they could beat the Russians?"

The beginning of the end. But when will the end finally come?

Miss Björk passes out the tests. Stephie's reflections come to an end when a piece of paper with purple type and the strong smell of duplicating fluid lands on her desk. She gets an encouraging smile along with it.

No one is allowed to start until all the tests have been distributed. They have three hours to solve the problems, from nine to noon.

Quickly, Stephie reads through the whole sheet. Eight problems. The first six are easy. Then there's a geometry question she's not sure about. Number eight is difficult, too, but as she reads through it a second time, something strikes her, and she knows how to solve it.

Eagerly, she gets out a piece of graph paper and picks up her pencil to begin her work. Before starting, though, she takes a quick look at May, who's sitting in the same row, over by the window.

May has the test in her hand and is holding it at arm's length, staring at the problems as if she's never seen any math before in her life. There's a big red blotch on each of her cheeks. Stephie can tell she's terrified. She wishes she could go over to May and tell her the problems aren't as hard as they look.

You can do the first six easy as pie, she'd like to say. *They're exactly the kind we've been practicing. Even if you make a mistake or two in working out the first six, you'll pass. Just don't freeze up. You'll be fine.*

But she's not allowed to leave her seat, and certainly not to talk. She can't help May get started. In fact, she can't even catch her eye.

Well, it won't do May any good if Stephie just sits there not getting started herself. So she reads problem eight one more time and decides to start with that one first.

An hour later, she is done with five of the problems. She has two of the easy ones left, and number seven, the hardest of all.

Miss Björk is walking around the auditorium. She stops by May and puts a hand on her shoulder. May looks up at her, her eyes pleading for help. Even though May's seat is several yards away, Stephie can see that she's perspiring.

What makes math so hard for May, who has such an easy time with all her other subjects?

Stephie does the two easy problems and tackles the tough one. She glances at the clock. Quarter to eleven.

16

She should have plenty of time to do the last problem and then make a clean ink copy of her work by noon.

A sob breaks the silence. Stephie looks up. May is sitting weeping, her head in her hands. Crumpled sheets of paper fall to the floor.

Miss Björk gets up from her seat at the front of the room and walks toward May, but before she gets there, May stands up and rushes to the door, crying her eyes out. Miss Björk watches her helplessly. She can't leave the auditorium unmonitored in the middle of a test.

Stephie hesitates only for a moment. Then she piles up her work, which, fortunately, is quite neat. She checks quickly that the answers to the seven problems she has finished are clear, and that it is possible to see how she has worked them out. She carries the papers to the front of the room, and gives them to Miss Björk, who is back in her seat.

"I'm finished," she says.

Miss Björk looks at the graph paper, full of penciled work. She leafs through the pile.

"Are you sure?" she asks.

"Yes," Stephie replies.

Miss Björk nods.

"All right, then," she says.

⁊

Stephie finds May on the basement stairs, outside the door marked BOMB SHELTER.

"I'll never pass," May sniffles. "I can't do it. I might as well quit school right now."

She turns her round face toward Stephie, her tears running and her eyes red. She holds her glasses in her hand.

"I have no idea what x times two and the square root of y is! Sometimes, in class, I think I understand, and when you explain things to me, too. But when I'm trying to do it alone, all the x's and y's turn into scary crawling bugs that I can't pin down. Don't you see?"

Stephie nods. "But you should have turned in what you'd done," she says. "The worst thing that could have happened would have been that your answers were wrong. And who knows, you might have gotten something right."

May has stopped crying now.

"Thanks a lot," she says. "That's it? That my answers were wrong? My answers were worse than wrong. They were an utter and complete disaster."

Stephie smiles. May sounds more like herself again.

"You'll have to talk to Miss Björk," says Stephie. "Maybe she can figure something out. You can't let a few little bugs keep you from getting into high school, can you?"

May smiles now, too, though one corner of her mouth gives a twitch, and her eyes still look miserable.

"No," she says. "No, I can't."

4

Every Wednesday night, Stephie and Vera, Stephie's friend from the island, meet at a café. Stephie feels a bit funny about spending her money on a luxury instead of adding something else to the food box for Mamma and Papa. But she feels just as funny about saying that to Vera, because then Vera would want to treat her every week.

Vera moved to the city about a year ago and has an income now. She's the housemaid for a family that lives in the center of town, quite near where Stephie lived when she boarded with her old friend Sven and his mother and father, when she first started grammar school. Vera is satisfied with the job. She has a nice little room of her own off the kitchen. The lady of the house is kind, and there are no kids to look after. Vera has Wednesday and Saturday evenings off, and all day Thursday. Lots of other girls have only one afternoon and one evening off each week, Vera explains to Stephie. She's gotten to know several girls who have domestic jobs, and they've told her.

Vera goes out dancing with them at Rota, the restaurant at the Liseberg Amusement Park. It's really called the Rotunda, but everybody says Rota, according to Vera. She's been nagging Stephie for months to get her to come along.

"We have *such* a good time," Vera says. "I think it would do you good to get out. All you ever do is sit and study."

That's not true. Stephie goes to the café with Vera, and she also goes to the movies, and sometimes to concerts. There's been a kind of unspoken pact between Stephie and Aunt Märta since the time two years ago when Miss Holm, the postmistress from the island, spotted Stephie outside a movie theater and almost got her thrown out of the Pentecostal congregation.

"I trust you to know the difference between right and wrong," Aunt Märta said at the time. "But if they decide to exclude you, I won't have any say in the matter."

When it comes to going out dancing, however, Stephie knows that would be crossing the line. Dancing is about as sinful as you can get.

Vera leans forward across the table.

"Stephie," she says. "What do you think could happen? Who might see you there? I've never, ever bumped into anyone from the island at Rota. Nobody's going to find you. And we'd have *such* a good time."

She gives Stephie a pleading look with those green eyes of hers. She's had her red hair cut to the latest fashion, shoulder length with a wave across the forehead. Still, Vera's hair always looks like it's trying to break free from its well-sculpted style and frizz up around her head, as it did when she and Stephie first became friends.

Vera thinks it's important to look like a young lady. They aren't kids anymore; Vera is sixteen. Not long ago, she boasted to Stephie that when she meets new people, she always tells them she's eighteen, and they believe her. Vera's breasts protrude under her tight sweater, she has red lipstick on, and in her dresser drawer are two pairs of silk stockings she saves to wear dancing.

Stephie is only four months younger than Vera, but she sometimes feels childish around her. She can tell she looks like a schoolgirl in her white blouses, her neatly buttoned cardigans, and her pleated skirts. She still has short hair, simply cut and with a side part. She doesn't very often think about her appearance, but when she's with Vera, she can hardly help it.

Vera is gorgeous. She was already pretty when they were in elementary school, but over the last six months she has blossomed into a real beauty. She could be on the cover of a magazine, Stephie thinks, or in a movie.

"I forgot to tell you!" Vera suddenly bursts out. "I'm getting my picture taken tomorrow."

"Where?"

Vera tells her all about it. The previous Saturday, at Rota, an "old man" came up to her. "Well, he wasn't all that old," she said, "maybe forty, but nobody over twenty-five goes dancing there." At first she found him a bit scary, but he was very polite, telling her he was a photographer with a studio of his own. He even gave her his business card, with his name and address embossed on it. He said she had the most fascinating face, explaining that he had lots of contacts at the magazines and would definitely be able to sell her picture to one of the big, glossy ones. After that, the sky was the limit for a pretty girl like her, he told her. He asked how old she was, and she said eighteen, as usual. That was when he gave her the business card and told her to stop by when she had time. Then he bowed and left.

"You know, he was quite good-looking," says Vera. "He was dark-haired, and had such a fine suit on."

Stephie feels her anxiety rising. There's something about Vera's story that doesn't add up.

"Do you really think you ought to go?" she begins.

Vera shrugs and laughs.

"Don't worry," she says. "He even said I could bring a girlfriend along if I liked. You don't happen to be free tomorrow at three?"

Stephie considers. She has German at three on Thursdays. Does she really dare tempt fate and Miss Krantz?

"Not really," she says. "I've got German class."

"Skip it!" says Vera. "You already know German. Keep me company!"

"Couldn't you go later? I'll be done by four."

"That won't work," says Vera. "He said it would take at least two hours, and I have to be back by six to do the dinner dishes."

"What if I came and met you there after school?"

"No," Vera replies. "I'd feel like a baby. As if I needed to be picked up. It would be different if you came along. Maybe he'd take your picture, too."

Stephie laughs. "I don't think I was meant to be a cover girl."

"You're very pretty," says Vera, "with your dark eyes and high cheekbones. All you need is a little makeup and a different hairdo. Come dancing on Saturday and I'll make you up!"

Her eyes gleam.

"Stop it," says Stephie. "You know I don't want to. And actually, I'm spending this weekend on the island."

They don't mention the photographer again. But on the tram back to Sandarna, Stephie's stomach tightens once more, just thinking about it.

5

"It would have been nice if you'd come along."

Stephie's in German class, listening to Miss Krantz going on and on about the uses of the conjunctive in German. She sneaks a peek at the watch Aunt Märta and Uncle Evert gave her for her fifteenth birthday. Ten after three.

Right now, Vera's in that photographer's studio, unless she had second thoughts. But that's not likely.

Vera wants to "be somebody," which means she either wants to become a film star or marry rich.

"'May you succeed in all you undertake!'" Miss Krantz says. "Translation, Ulla?"

Stephie imagines a photograph of Vera, head cocked, eyes sparkling beneath the wave across her forehead.

When May's mother comes home at five-thirty, the table is set and dinner is ready. Stephie is exhausted. Before Auntie Tyra even gets to take off her coat, she has to comfort Ninni and bark at Erik for having ruined Gunnel's paper dolls. Kurre and Olle vanished with their marbles as soon as they heard her footsteps coming up the stairs.

The sausages are a little crisp and the horseradish sauce lumpy. But the potatoes are boiled just right.

"What's up?" Auntie Tyra asks. "You look so worried. Not had bad news from your parents, I hope?"

"No," says Stephie. "No, in fact they got that box I sent."

Stephie wishes she could confide in Auntie Tyra. She's the kind of person who always seems to know what to do, and even starts doing it before anyone else has time to think. In spite of her heavy body and her frequent complaints that her back and knees hurt, she's almost never sitting down, and she's almost always cheerful. Even when she loses her temper, she sounds as if she's just pretending to be angry. And no matter how busy she is, she always has a clear, calm look in her eyes.

Those eyes are now focused on Stephie.

"I certainly hope no one's been treating you badly. If they are, they'll have me to contend with, I can tell you that!"

Stephie can't help laughing. Auntie Tyra makes it sound as though Stephie's just a kid, like Erik and Gunnel.

"No, no," she says. "I'm just tired. We've got so much homework."

The moment passes. What could she have said to Auntie Tyra about Vera, anyway? It's too late now. She didn't go along to the photographer's with Vera, and she didn't stop her from going, either.

"Kurre and Olle!" Auntie Tyra calls. "You two are in charge of the dishes. Stephanie has homework to do."

The younger boys grumble, but do as they are told.

How could Stephie have stopped her? Vera wanted to go, and maybe this is her chance for a better life.

"But if I were you, Vera," Stephie mutters to herself, "I wouldn't have gone."

6

Just before six o'clock, Stephie runs down to the Co-Op to phone Vera. But the line is busy, and the shop is about to close. Stephie tries three times as the girl behind the counter becomes increasingly impatient. When the line stays busy, Stephie has to give up.

The next day, she goes to the tobacconist's near school on her lunch break to try again. This time the phone rings, but there's no answer. And the minute school ends, she has to take the tram down to the Wood Pier to catch the boat out to the island. They have Saturday off this week, so Stephie will be spending an unusually long weekend with Aunt Märta and Uncle Evert.

෴

Stephie stands out on deck, watching the islands and skerries pass. The sun shines on the granite cliffs, making them gleam in hundreds of shades of gray, brown, and pink, bright against the blue sea. The bushes and stunted trees growing up out of the cracks between the stones are surrounded by a maze of light green vegetation. Here and there, purple bunches of wild pansies glitter.

She remembers her first boat trip to the island, when everything just looked gray. Now her eyes can distinguish the colors of the archipelago.

There's no one in the harbor to meet her, but her red bicycle is leaning up against Uncle Evert's boathouse. Someone has thoughtfully saved her the trouble of carrying her heavy schoolbag and her bag of dirty laundry all the way across the island.

The thoughtfulness warms Stephie's heart. She feels even happier when she sees the *Diana* tied up along the jetty. That means Uncle Evert is at home. The last time she visited the island, she didn't even see him. Leading the life of a fisherman often means being at sea for a week or more. One's return depends on the weather, the winds, and now, what with the war, the presence or absence of foreign warships.

Stephie straps her book bag to the clamp and hangs her laundry bag from the handlebars. Throwing a leg over the frame, she bikes off through the village and past the yellow house where Nellie lives. She'll visit with

Nellie and Auntie Alma tomorrow, if not this very evening.

The wind is mild on her face, and the bicycle rolls easily. Now that Stephie has learned to ride a bike, she can hardly remember how difficult it was at first. But every time she passes a certain turn in the road, she recalls one time, long ago, when Vera rescued her from the ditch.

Stephie and May have been talking about starting to ride their bikes to school to save on tram fares. Stephie could take her bicycle to Göteborg, and May could get a used one. But Stephie doesn't really like the idea of biking in city traffic, so she is secretly pleased that May can't seem to save up for a bicycle.

Coasting down the last slope, Stephie comes to a halt at the gate. Aunt Märta is outside, hanging laundry. Most of the clothes are Uncle Evert's fishing things, heavy blue overalls and plaid shirts.

"Here I come, bringing more laundry!" Stephie calls out, waving her bag.

Aunt Märta turns around and gives a wave, a clothespin in her hand. Stephie parks her bike and joins her at the washing line. Lifting a shirt from the basket, she hangs it next to the one Aunt Märta is hanging, taking clothespins from the little cloth bag around Aunt Märta's waist.

Their shoulders rub. That's about as close as anyone ever gets to Aunt Märta.

"Thank you so much for bringing the bike," says Stephie.

"Nellie did it," Aunt Märta tells her. "She and Alma were here yesterday, and I asked her to ride it down to the boathouse and leave it there for you. Her bike is still here. You can ride it back to Alma's tomorrow, and then walk home afterward."

Stephie turns around and sees Nellie's blue bike by the outbuilding. She can hardly believe her little sister rides such a big bike now.

"You *will* be going to see them tomorrow, won't you?" Aunt Märta goes on.

She makes it sound urgent, as if there were something hidden in those words.

"Sure," says Stephie. "I was planning on it. Maybe even this evening."

"No," Aunt Märta tells her. "Wait until tomorrow. Uncle Evert and I want you all to ourselves tonight."

Stephie feels her heart rise. It amazes her that Aunt Märta, the same stern, strict Aunt Märta she was so intimidated by when she first came to the island, talks to her like this! She'd like to give her a hug, but she knows Aunt Märta would only shrug her off with some line about being too emotional.

When Stephie lifts a second shirt from the laundry basket, Aunt Märta scolds her. "There's no need for you to be hanging up laundry before you've even changed out of your city clothes," she says. "You go on in and see your uncle Evert."

Uncle Evert is at the kitchen table, sitting with a cup of coffee and the newspaper. He stands up when she comes in.

"Stephie," he says. "It's been much too long!"

He pats her cheek. Uncle Evert isn't given to hugging, either.

Stephie takes out a cup and sits across from him. She pours herself some of the brown liquid from the coffeepot. She's learned to drink coffee here in Sweden, though of course it isn't real coffee. Real coffee is rationed, and saved for special occasions. Their everyday "coffee" is a bitter chicory surrogate.

Uncle Evert watches her movements between the sugar bowl and her cup.

"Lucky Märta didn't see you do that," he says. "She's being extra careful with sugar—well, with everything that's being rationed. No more than one cube per cup, that's the rule."

"Well, if I only have every other cup," says Stephie, "then I can put two cubes in mine!"

Uncle Evert laughs. "Every other cup! Aren't you the clever one?"

"How's the fishing going?"

"Same as always," Uncle Evert tells her. "We fetch a good price for whatever we manage to catch. But we often come home with lots of space in the hold. The German ships hound us out of our fishing grounds. Not to mention worrying about hitting a mine . . ."

He goes silent. But Stephie knows. Mines have blown

35

up twelve Swedish fishing vessels since the start of the war. Nearly fifty crew members have been killed.

"We have no choice," Uncle Evert adds. "We've got to fish, don't we? What would we live off otherwise?"

Uncle Evert's large hands are resting on the tabletop. The long scar along the bottom of his left thumb stands out white against his suntan. Stephie wishes she could reach out and touch him, but she knows he wouldn't like it.

"We're heading out on the *Diana* again tomorrow," he tells her.

"Tomorrow? But I've just come home!"

"I know," he says. "But the navy's asked us for help. Every available fishing boat is turning out. One of the Swedish submarines—the *Wolf*—has been missing since last Thursday. It disappeared during a maneuver. We're going to throw our nets and see if we can locate it on the seabed."

"What about the crew?" Stephie asks breathlessly.

"They may still be alive," Uncle Evert tells her. "There's still a chance. While there's life, there's hope."

Aunt Märta comes in with the empty laundry basket. She sits down at the table and pours herself a cup of coffee, too. Then she lifts a sugar cube from the bowl, breaking it in two and returning half to the bowl. Stephie's and Uncle Evert's eyes meet. They smile.

"Have you heard anything from your parents?" Aunt Märta asks.

"Yes, there was a card from Mamma this week. She sent her best regards and asked me to thank you for the package."

"Any news?" Uncle Evert asks.

"She's going to sing in an opera. The Queen of the Night in *The Magic Flute*!"

"An opera?" Aunt Märta says, sounding incredulous. "There? At the camp?"

Stephie nods. "That's what she wrote."

Uncle Evert looks pensive. "Maybe so," he says. "Maybe that's exactly the kind of thing they have to do at the camps. To be able to go on being human."

Stephie looks right into Uncle Evert's eyes—eyes as blue and as deep as the sea.

"Yes," she says. "I think so, too."

7

On Saturday morning when Stephie wakes up, a ray of sun is peeking in through her little gable window. Her room is nestled just under the eaves. She stretches, looking around her. On the dresser is the photo of her whole family on an outing in the Wienerwald. She brought the portraits of her parents to May's, where they hang over her bed. She wants them near her. But nowadays, since she shares a room with May and her sisters, she no longer talks to Mamma and Papa in their frames, as she used to.

Stephie gazes at the photograph. Mamma, Papa, Nellie, and herself. She remembers how her father asked a nice older man to take the picture for him, so they could all be in it. How hard it was to get Nellie to stop playing and stand still for a minute. How Mamma made a joke about Papa, that he ought to have been wearing his hiking boots and have a feather in his hat.

"You look like you got lost on your way to the office, even though we're on a walk in the woods," Mamma had said, laughing.

They made another outing to the Wienerwald, just a year later. Only, when they got off the tram at the last stop, Neuwaldegg, men in brown uniforms were standing there. One of them stopped Papa.

"Go back into town," the man in brown ordered him roughly. "We don't want any Jews poisoning the fresh air out here. The Wienerwald is for Austrians."

Papa faltered, lurching back as if he had been slapped across the face.

At that very moment, Mamma burst into an Austrian folk song. People stopped to listen. Many smiled. Two young girls joined in.

Mamma sang the whole song, all the way to the very end. Then, taking Stephie and Nellie by the hand, she turned around and went back to their seats on the tram. Papa followed them.

That was their last outing to the Wienerwald.

❧

"Only the nobility have breakfast this late in the day," Aunt Märta says ironically when Stephie, finally dressed and ready, appears at the kitchen door. But it doesn't bother her. She hears the smile behind the words.

Once she's had her breakfast, Stephie calls Vera's

number again. This time, Vera picks up, but her voice sounds peculiar, and she says she can't talk now. Stephie assumes there are other people around. They agree to meet as usual on Wednesday evening, and hang up.

"Is there something wrong with Vera?" Aunt Märta asks.

"Not really," says Stephie. "She was busy, that's all."

"That child could use some looking after," Aunt Märta says. "She shouldn't be blowing around the city, from pillar to post."

"Well, she does have a job."

"I believe you know what I mean," says Aunt Märta.

Uncle Evert has gone down to the harbor to check on the *Diana* and hear if there's any news. The harbor's where you go if you want to know the latest, both about the island and about the world at large—or you go to see Miss Holm at the post office.

Aunt Märta is putting cans and boxes on the kitchen table. She's already got a brown cardboard box ready, too.

"Let's organize the package," she says. "Then you can send it when you go into the village."

They work together, packing oatmeal and flour, canned meats and dried prunes, tins of peas, and a bottle of cod liver oil.

"Ugh," says Stephie.

"It's good for you, though," says Aunt Märta. "I'm sure they need the vitamins."

The last thing Aunt Märta does is to take a small

glass jar and fill it with sugar. Stephie looks at her in surprise. Their precious, rationed sugar?

"Right, that ought to do it," Aunt Märta says, hiding the jar of sugar deep down below the other goods. "That's everything, I think."

She closes the box, tying it up sturdily with string. Stephie writes the address label. *Frau Elisabeth Steiner, Block C III, Theresienstadt.* Papa and Mamma have separate addresses at the camp. Apparently not even married couples are allowed to live together. Stephie wishes she knew more about what Mamma and Papa's life in the camp is like. How often they see each other, how they spend their days, whether Mamma makes meals for Papa out of the things Stephie sends.

Stephie ties the box to the back of Nellie's bike with a leather strap. It's so heavy she can't manage to ride up the hill and has to get off and push the bike.

When Stephie arrives at the post office, Miss Holm is talkative as usual.

"Stephie!" she says, clapping her hands. "It's been ages! Just think, I remember as if it were yesterday the first time you came in here with Mrs. Jansson. I think you wanted a stamp, didn't you? And here you are, all grown up. Grammar school girl, at that."

Stephie gives her the box, and Miss Holm weighs it. The postage costs nearly as much as the things inside it. The only way to send anything to Theresienstadt is by registered mail.

"So what about Vera Hedberg?" Miss Holm asks. "She lives in the city now, too. Are you still such good friends?"

"Yes," says Stephie.

The best way to deal with Miss Holm is to say as little as possible. She repeats everything she hears, usually with more than a little exaggeration.

It's not far from the post office to Auntie Alma and Uncle Sigurd's house. Elsa and John, Nellie's foster sister and brother, are playing in the yard, but there is no sign of Nellie. Stephie parks Nellie's bike and knocks. Auntie Alma opens the door.

"Stephie!" she exclaims. "I'm so glad to see you. Come on in. Nellie's upstairs. You go on up if you like. Bring Nellie down. I've got sweet rolls and juice for you."

Stephie goes up the stairs. Auntie Alma and Uncle Sigurd's house has three upstairs bedrooms, a big one for the grown-ups and two smaller ones. Nellie used to have one of them to herself, with Elsa and John in the other. Now Elsa and Nellie share.

The door to the girls' room is shut. Stephie knocks, then opens it. The minute she steps inside, she can feel that something has changed, and not only because Elsa's bed is here now, on the wall opposite Nellie's.

Nellie is sitting on the edge of her bed. She looks sullen. Stephie sits down next to her and takes her hand. Nellie goes stiff.

Stephie wonders what's wrong, but she knows Nellie well enough not to ask outright.

"I like your dress," she says instead. "Is it new? Did Auntie Alma make it?"

"'I like your dress,'" Nellie mimics her nastily. "Do you think I'm still seven or something?"

"I was only saying you look pretty in it," Stephie replies.

Nellie is really very pretty, with her long black braids, rosy cheeks, and big, dark eyes.

"Pretty!" says Nellie. "With this hair?"

"What's wrong with your hair?"

"Well, maybe it's all right to go around looking like a gypsy in the city, but not here! I wish I looked like everybody else. Fair hair and blue eyes. I wish I were Swedish!"

"Are you being teased?"

Stephie remembers being bullied by Sylvia the first year she lived on the island. But Nellie's always been very popular at school.

"No," says Nellie. "But I can see with my own eyes. I look like a changeling. Can't you tell?"

Nellie points to a photo on the dresser. It's from a photographer's studio, and very recent. Auntie Alma and Uncle Sigurd are sitting next to each other. John is on Auntie Alma's lap. Elsa is standing next to her, leaning against her. They all have open, round faces with light-colored eyes and blond hair. Nellie is standing

43

behind them. In their company, she looks like an exotic plant, a princess out of the *Arabian Nights*.

"How can you say something so unfair?" Stephie asks. "Auntie Alma has always treated you as if you were her own child."

"I wish I was!"

"How can you say that? You have parents of your own, or have you forgotten?"

Nellie doesn't reply, just shrugs. Stephie feels like taking her by the shoulders and giving her a shake. She'd like to shake her sister until the old lively, warmhearted Nellie comes out of this grumpy stranger with her closed-up face.

That's when she sees what's different about the room.

Nellie's portraits of Mamma and Papa—the same ones Stephie has—are missing. They've always been on the dresser, where the new family photo is now.

"Where did you put your pictures?" Stephie asks. "Of Mamma and Papa?"

"In my drawer," Nellie tells her glumly.

"Why?"

"This is Elsa's room now, too. I don't think she wants to look at them all the time."

"Did she say that?"

"No."

"Nellie," says Stephie. "They're our parents. Your parents. I don't want you to forget that. You do write to them, don't you?"

"Sure I do. I write once a week. Alternate weeks to Mamma and Papa. Any other questions?"

Nellie's voice is harsh. As if she feels the need to defend herself. As if Stephie were her enemy.

Stephie goes down on her knees in front of Nellie. She takes her hands and tries to hold her gaze.

At that very moment, Auntie Alma calls them.

"Stephie! Nellie! Come have some juice."

Nellie pushes Stephie away and stands up.

"Auntie Alma's calling," she says. "I'm going down."

❧

Stephie politely declines to stay for sweet rolls and juice. She knows Auntie Alma will be offended, but she can't just sit there pretending. She needs to be by herself, now that Nellie doesn't want to talk to her anymore.

Take care of Nellie. She can hear her father's voice from the railroad station in Vienna, the last time they saw each other, nearly four years ago. *Take care of Nellie.* Both Papa and Mamma write that to her often. *Take care of Nellie. She's so young.*

Stephie has let her parents down. She should never have agreed to go to grammar school in the city. She and Nellie ought to have stuck together. And she's the one who bears the responsibility since she's older.

Maybe she shouldn't start high school, for Nellie's sake? But if she doesn't continue her education, she'll have to get a job. And there are no jobs for girls on the island. The girls here do as Vera has done, take domestic jobs in the city, or work in the factories. Unless they marry fishermen and stay on the island.

It's too late, anyway.

She can't take care of Nellie anymore, because Nellie is never again going to let her.

8

Before taking the boat back to Göteborg on Sunday evening, Stephie asks Aunt Märta to phone the relief committee to find out whether they will pay her room and board for another three years, while she's in high school. Aunt Märta promises.

On her way back, Stephie stands out on deck again, but this time, she mostly just stares down into the water. The surface of the sea is unruffled and gleaming. Somewhere at the bottom, in the depths, might be the missing submarine, the *Wolf*.

That night she dreams that she has been shut up in a narrow room with some other people. There's almost no air. She wakes up feeling as if she is suffocating.

On Wednesday, Miss Björk is at her desk at the front of the room, a pile of test papers before her, gazing out at the class. Thirty-four pair of eyes meet hers—nervous, pleading, or self-confident. Then there is May, who just stares down at her desktop.

"Your test results," says Miss Björk, "aren't exactly brilliant. No one had a perfect score this time. On the other hand, no one who turned in a test paper failed, though there are a few borderline cases. I'm not going to keep you in suspense. Ulla, would you return the test papers, please?"

The class monitor walks forward to the teacher's desk and collects the pile. One by one, she returns the tests. A few of the girls leaf eagerly through theirs. Others try to look unperturbed. Stephie just glances at hers. She already knows that she got 28 out of 32. That will give her an A-minus. She would have had an A if she'd done that last problem. But she couldn't do it without letting May down.

Stephie looks toward May, but May's eyes are still glued to her desktop.

"And then we have May," says Miss Björk. "You didn't turn in a test paper. I assume you fell ill during the exam?"

May looks up. Her lips are moving, but no sound comes out.

"Isn't that right?" asks Miss Björk. "You certainly did look ill to me. So I've decided not to count this test toward your grade. But if I am going to be able to give you a final grade, you are going to have to prove that you did your work on this section of the course. I've made up an extra assignment for you. I'll give you two weeks to do it at home. Come see me in the staff room on your lunch break today, and we'll look through it together."

May's lips are moving again, but it's like watching an old silent movie. Stephie can read her lips, though. May is saying, *Thank you, Miss Björk.*

≈

After her lunchtime talk with Miss Björk, May is bright and chipper again. Their teacher has promised to pass May in math if she does her extra assignment diligently.

" 'On one condition,' she said," May tells Stephie.

"What condition?"

"That I apply for the classics program in high school and never take any math again. As if I'd do anything else!"

"So we won't be classmates next year," says Stephie.

"No, that's too bad." May puts her arm around Stephie's shoulders. "But we'll always be best friends. No matter what."

≈

On their way home from school, Stephie and May split up outside the Co-Op. May's going to pick up Ninni and Erik, while Stephie's going to phone Aunt Märta from the store and then shop for dinner.

The phone rings and rings before Aunt Märta answers.

"Jansson residence," she says at last.

"It's me," says Stephie. "Aunt Märta, were you able to call the relief committee?"

There's a moment of silence. Then she speaks.

"Yes, I did."

"What did they say?"

Silence again.

"Do you really think you need to go on to high school, dear?" Stephie hears.

"Was that what they asked?"

"They said most of the refugee children your age are already earning their keep," says Aunt Märta. "It's hard for them to collect money now. Everyone needs everything they have. They said they could offer you one more year of school. That would get you a junior secondary degree, and a good office job. Maybe you could eventually study nursing. Nursing students have free room and board while they're in training."

Stephie's hand is gripping the black receiver tightly. She has to hold on to something.

"And what did you say, Aunt Märta?"

"That it sounded like a sensible plan. Girls always end up getting married, in any case. Of course, schooling's a fine thing, but high school won't prepare you for a profession. High school won't get you a better job."

"But you know I want to be a doctor," Stephie says softly. "You know that, Aunt Märta."

"My dear girl," Aunt Märta says. "Times being what they are, I think you're going to have to put such fancies out of your mind."

Stephie can tell she's about to cry. She feels the girl behind the counter staring at her in curiosity. So she brings the conversation to an end, pays, and leaves.

She sits down on a bench by a sandbox between the houses. She hadn't expected this. When a way was finally found for her to go on to grammar school, she had assumed there would be no question that she would go to high school, too.

Junior secondary diploma. Office job. Nurse's training. That wasn't the future she had envisaged for herself. Nor the one Mamma and Papa had imagined for her, either.

Her old bitterness rises. If Anna-Lisa, Aunt Märta's and Uncle Evert's own daughter, hadn't died at the age of twelve, if she had wanted to go on to high school, surely they would have let her. They would have been proud to have such a gifted daughter. But a foster child is a different matter.

Stephie's been sitting on the bench for twenty minutes when she realizes that May is waiting for the dinner groceries. The groceries she's forgotten all about buying!

She goes back to the Co-Op, trying not to notice the sympathetic gaze of the shop assistant. When the girl asks Stephie if everything is all right, Stephie answers curtly.

"Of course."

❧

Stephie doesn't say anything to May as they make dinner and eat. She just can't right now, not with all the kids around. After that, she has to go out. Vera is expecting her at the café. For once, Stephie's not looking forward to her Wednesday evening. She'd much rather take a walk with May and talk about their future school situations.

Vera's already there when Stephie arrives. She's a bit pale, but her lips are defiantly red. They each order a cup of coffee and an iced almond cake.

Stephie just can't keep it to herself any longer. The whole story, beginning with the relief committee and Aunt Märta, and on to her dreams of finishing high school, run right out of her, a long stream of words.

"And then she says girls always just get married anyhow!" Stephie finishes indignantly.

"Well, you will get married, won't you?"

"I might, but not until I've become a doctor," says Stephie.

"That's sure stingy of the Janssons," says Vera. "I'm sure they could afford to keep you in school themselves, since it's so important to you. They're quite well off."

Stephie doesn't reply. She may very well have been thinking the same thing herself just a little while ago, but she'd never criticize Aunt Märta and Uncle Evert in front of Vera.

"How did it go with that photographer?" she asks to change the subject.

Vera stirs her coffee, staring down into the vortex she's created in the brown liquid.

"All right."

Vera is never so short with Stephie.

"All right?"

"Yes. He took three rolls, and promised to send them to *Look* magazine this week."

"Will you get to see them?"

Vera shrugs. "I don't know that I want to."

Stephie's very confused. "You don't want to see them?"

"Forget it," says Vera. "Let's talk about something nice now. Are you coming along to Rota on Saturday? Please?"

Suddenly Stephie realizes how angry she is with Aunt Märta. Angry with all her rules and all her preconceptions about how a life should be lived. About girls just getting married. About it being sinful to go out dancing.

Why should she obey Aunt Märta's rules? Why

should she pay any attention to a god who forbids every bit of fun? Just a couple of hours ago, she would have answered *For Aunt Märta's sake*. But now she doesn't care about Aunt Märta's sake.

"Yes," she says. "I'll come. If you'll lend me something to wear."

9

Miss Björk can tell immediately that something's not right. After biology class the next morning, she asks Stephie to help her carry the posters back up to the map room.

"What's the matter?" she asks with concern.

"The relief committee said no," says Stephie. "They won't pay for high school. They'll let me do a fourth year so I can get a junior secondary degree, but that's it."

Miss Björk frowns. Then she grins.

"Wow, then I'll get to have you for another year! I'm not qualified to teach high school, you know. I'm nothing but a poor young secondary schoolmistress."

She hangs the posters of the internal organs of the human body back where they belong.

"But seriously," she says. "Was that a final decision?"

"I think so. It sounded that way."

"Did you talk to them yourself?"

"No, Aunt Märta called."

"And what did she say?"

"That girls just get married. That I could study nursing after a while."

Miss Björk sighs. "When I hear things like that," she says, "I realize how fortunate I've been. Of all the pupils at my all-girl grammar school, I was the only one who got to graduate from high school and go on to further education. It was all thanks to my mother. She wanted to go to university but ended up at teacher's seminary. I thought things had changed, though, over the last twenty years. That people's prejudices about women—"

She stops herself short.

"Well, I'm sure the last thing you want is a lecture on women's rights just now," she says. "And besides, the bell's about to ring. Let me think on this one a bit. I bet I'll figure something out. Come have tea with me on Sunday afternoon, and we'll talk it through. Two o'clock?"

"Thank you," says Stephie. "Thank you so much, Miss Björk."

⁊

Vera finishes at six on Saturdays. At a quarter after, Stephie knocks at the kitchen door and Vera opens it, her hair in rollers.

"Come on in," she says, pulling Stephie into her little

maid's room off the kitchen. "My employers are invited out to dinner, but they haven't left yet."

On the bed in Vera's room is a newly ironed dress. It's green with little white dots, buttons down the front, and shoulder pads.

"Do you like it?"

"It's gorgeous," says Stephie. "But don't you want to wear it yourself?"

Vera points to a blue-flowered dress hanging from the drapery rod that separates the sink from the rest of the room.

"I'll wear that one. Now let's get started on your hair. I think you ought to take your blouse off."

Vera washes Stephie's hair in the sink behind the curtain, and puts it in rollers. Then she plucks Stephie's eyebrows with little tweezers. It hurts, but Stephie grits her teeth and bears it.

Next, Vera looks critically at Stephie's white undershirt. She pulls a brassiere out of a dresser drawer.

"This is probably too big," she says. "But we'll stuff it with these old, worn-out stockings."

Stephie removes her undershirt. She's a bit embarrassed about her breasts. Stephie puts on the brassiere, and Vera stuffs one stocking in each bra cup, arranging them carefully so they look natural.

"No one will ever know once you have the dress on," she says.

Vera puts a little rouge on Stephie's cheeks, powders them over, and puts red lipstick on her lips.

While Vera's doing her own makeup and brushing out her curls, Stephie examines herself in the mirror. With red on her lips, she can suddenly see a resemblance to Mamma. *Vera may be right,* she thinks. *I just might be pretty.*

She purses her lips and tries to blink like a movie star, so her eyelashes brush her cheeks.

But when Vera turns around with her billowing curls and smiling mouth, Stephie knows Vera has something she doesn't. A gleam in her eyes, a sheen to her complexion, and something about her hair. Stephie can't put a name to it.

When Stephie's hair has dried, Vera removes the rollers and arranges it in soft curls around her face. She brushes up her slanting bangs, putting in a bobby pin so they form a little roll across her forehead.

"There you are," Vera says, satisfied. "See how much older you look?"

Vera lends Stephie a garter and one of her pairs of silk stockings.

"Be careful with them," Vera warns. "It's really expensive to get them mended if they run."

Lastly, they put on the dresses. They walk out into the empty apartment to examine themselves in the big hall mirror with a gold frame. One blue body with red-gold hair, one green one with black curls. Vera puts an arm around Stephie's waist.

"Do you see now?" she asks. "See how pretty you are?"

She opens the door to one of the rooms.

"Come on," she says. "Now I'm going to teach you to dance."

Vera turns on the big radio gramophone, turning the dials until she finds a station that plays modern dance music. Stephie's a bit uncomfortable.

"Are you . . . I mean are we allowed to be in here?"

"What they don't know won't hurt them," Vera tells her. "We're not going to do any harm. Just dance a little. May I have this dance, miss?"

"Yes, thank you," Stephie answers, playing along.

Vera teaches Stephie how to position her arms. Left hand on her partner's shoulder, right hand in his.

"We'll start with the two-step," says Vera.

The two-step's easy. All Stephie has to do is follow Vera's movements.

"Head up a bit," Vera instructs her. "That's it. Do you come here often, miss?"

"No," says Stephie. "This is my first time."

"That's what I thought," Vera tells her. "I would have noticed a beauty like you if you'd been here before."

The music fades. Vera bows.

"Thank you for the dance. May I have the next one as well?"

They wait until the radio plays a fast swing melody. Vera takes Stephie by the hand.

"Just follow," she says. "The man always leads. Let him spin you around, and just follow."

With a tug, she pulls Stephie toward her, placing an

arm around her waist. Then she pushes Stephie away again, out onto the floor, but without letting go of her hand. Stephie spins and flies, whirls, and dances across the floor. Suddenly she collides with a chair, loses her balance, and falls.

"Are you all right?" Vera asks.

"I think I'm fine."

"Sorry, I'm not accustomed to leading, you know. I guess I was too rough. I really hope I didn't hurt you."

Stephie smooths down her dress. "How do I look?" she asks.

"A bit ruffled," says Vera. "It's time to fix ourselves up and get going. Rota opens at eight, so we ought to be there then. It gets awfully crowded later. And we'll want a table close to the dance floor."

Vera fixes Stephie's hair and her own. They get their coats from Vera's room and are about to leave when Vera catches sight of Stephie's sensible, flat shoes with laces.

"Oh, no! You can't be seen in those shoes!" she cries. "What are we going to do?"

Vera's shoes are sixes and Stephie wears fives. Even if Vera had two pairs of dancing shoes, Stephie couldn't borrow one.

Vera's frown only lasts a moment. "Hang on," she says.

She vanishes, returning shortly with a pair of high-heeled shoes in hand.

"Where did you get those?"

"They're my mistress's."

"You're crazy. What if I ruin them?"

"Just take a look!"

She pulls Stephie into one of the bedrooms. There's a big double bed. Vera opens a closet. From floor to ceiling, there are shoe boxes, piles and piles of shoe boxes.

"You don't really think she can keep track of all her shoes, do you? I took a pair from the very bottom, one she never wears. Let's go!"

10

By the time they get to Rota, it's ten to eight and there's already a line. They wait their turn, buy tickets, and are finally in the lobby, hanging up their coats. The dance music is playing inside.

Vera gives Stephie a smile. "Ready?"

Now Stephie sees what gave the place the name Rotunda. The huge dance floor is circular. There's a fountain in the middle, surrounded by flower arrangements. Above the fountain is an enormous chandelier. Along the walls are raised galleries with little tables. On the stage is the band, eleven white-tuxedoed men. Everything is glittering and twinkling.

"Oooh" is all Stephie can manage.

Vera makes her way to one of the tables.

"Right by the dance floor and really close to the band," she whispers to Stephie. "Where everybody can see us."

They take their table, and Vera orders them soft drinks and cream cake. Stephie gives her a strange look. Vera almost never eats cream cake. At the café, she's always saying she needs to think about her figure.

Vera notices her gaze.

"It's different here," she says. "If you have a piece of cream cake in front of you, the boys know you aren't worried about gaining weight. And nobody says you have to finish it."

A young man with glasses asks Vera to dance almost right away. Stephie sips her soft drink, pokes around at her cake, and keeps an eye on Vera's blue dress, watching the skirt twirl around and around. When will it be her turn?

She lets her eyes wander around the room. Groups of boys stand here and there, leaning nonchalantly against the walls, hands in their trouser pockets. But all the girls are seated. So many pretty girls waiting to be asked to dance. Why would anyone notice her?

After two dances, the young man accompanies Vera back to the table, pulls her chair out for her, and bows.

"What a bore!" Vera whispers as he walks away. "And not much of a dancer, either. Between songs, he couldn't think of a single thing to say. Not so much as a 'Do you come here often?' "

Someone asks Vera to dance again. After that, she just dances and dances. Stephie starts to regret having come along. She doesn't want to sit there like a wall-flower until it's time to go home.

Then the young man with the glasses comes back. He may have wanted to ask Vera to dance again, but, seeing Stephie alone, he bows politely.

"May I have this dance?" he asks.

At last! Stephie doesn't mind at all that Vera dismissed him as boring. She follows him to the dance floor.

He really isn't much of a dancer. Twice he almost steps on Stephie's toes. He blushes furiously each time, apologizing profusely.

They have two dances in a row without exchanging more than a couple of words. Then he walks her back to her seat.

So that was it. Her Saturday-evening fun.

There are more and more couples on the dance floor now, and fewer and fewer girls at the tables. Everyone must notice her sitting by herself, dance after dance.

Stephie puts a bite of cake in her mouth. The cream has already gone stiff and dry, but at least eating makes her look occupied.

Then Vera arrives with two young men in tow. She's holding one by the hand, and the other is walking behind them.

"May I introduce you?" she asks. "This is Bengt and Rikard. My girlfriend Stephie."

Stephie extends a hand. Rikard, the one who was holding Vera's hand, is tall and fair and good-looking. Bengt is shorter, wide-shouldered, and less handsome. But he has lovely gray eyes.

They sit down at the girls' table.

"Ah, I see you haven't had time to eat tonight, either," Rikard says, glancing at Vera's untouched piece of cake.

They seem to have met before.

"That's right," Vera replies. "Which is too bad, since the whipped cream has already dried up."

She pushes her plate away.

Bengt turns to Stephie. "Vera tells me you're from Vienna," he says. "Excuse me for being nosy, but how did you end up here?"

Stephie hesitates. She certainly can't tell her whole story to someone she's just met. Not here. It would spoil everybody's evening.

"Stephie's a refugee," Vera answers for her. "She's Jewish."

Vera gives Bengt a look. Stephie can see that she's trying to say *No more questions.* Bengt quickly changes the subject.

"I've never seen you here before," he says. "Do you come often?"

"No," says Stephie. "This is my first time."

"Would you like to dance?"

"Yes, thank you."

Bengt is a good dancer. He leads her calmly and confidently on the dance floor, a firm hand on her waist. It feels good having his arm around her, and the hand holding hers is large and warm. Even when Bengt spins her out across the floor, she feels secure, knowing that he'll pull her back, like a boomerang.

Vera and Rikard are dancing nearby. Rikard lifts Vera, spinning her upside down. Vera's skirt falls back across her upper body, revealing her white underwear and her garters.

Bengt smiles when he sees Stephie's look.

"We'll take things a bit easier, you and me," he says. "Right?"

You and me. As if they belong together.

Stephie doesn't really know how it's happened, but suddenly it's midnight and Rota is closing. They've been dancing and talking all evening, Vera and Rikard, she and Bengt. Bengt asked Stephie her age, but before she could open her mouth, Vera answered.

"Seventeen."

So later, when he asks Stephie about school, she has to pretend she's a sophomore in high school. Bengt graduated from the business high school and is now apprenticed to one of Sweden's big companies. Rikard is a technical illustrator at a construction firm, studying engineering at night school.

Now they're outside and about to go their separate ways. Unless, of course, the boys want to walk them home. She certainly can't expect Bengt to walk her all the way out to Sandarna, though. He lives in Mölndal, the other direction altogether.

"You don't want to go home yet, do you?" Rikard says. "It's just midnight. You girls don't have to be home any particular time, right?"

Stephie shakes her head. She told May and her parents she might sleep over at Vera's, so they won't worry about her.

"My employers are at a dinner party," Vera says. "They tend to get back late, and sleep late the next morning. They won't notice what time I come in."

"That settles it," says Rikard. "I've got the key to my parents' cabin. It's not very far away. Do you want to come?"

"Sure," says Vera. "All right, Stephie?"

Stephie has her doubts. Going along with two boys in the middle of the night? Well, Vera knows them. And she obviously wants to go, but not by herself. If Stephie says no, she'll spoil things for Vera, who has gone out of her way to show Stephie a good time.

"All right," she says. "I guess."

11

They get to the cabin by bus, jolting slowly along a narrow country road. It's late and dark, and after they get off the bus, they have to walk through the woods. Bengt takes Stephie's arm to keep her from stumbling in her high heels. She's a bit worried about the shoes, but she decides there isn't much she can do now. Bengt's steady grip on her arm makes her feel more secure.

Rikard's parents' cabin is on a hillside in an allotment, an area of community gardens, each with a tiny cabin almost playhouse-sized. The dark forest looms behind the rows of cottages, and a pale moon hangs above the treetops. The air is perfumed with the scent of flowering trees and newly mowed grass. There are lights in a couple of the cabins, but most are silent and dark. Singing can be heard coming from one over at the far end.

Rikard unlocks the door to a green wooden cabin in the row nearest the woods. The others settle down in rattan furniture on the glassed-in porch while Rikard gets four glasses, takes out a pocket flask, and pours the transparent liquid.

"Cheers, everybody!" he says.

They all raise their glasses. Stephie takes a little sip. It burns her mouth. Rikard and Bengt drink all of theirs, and Rikard pours refills. Stephie's uncomfortable, but Bengt's gray eyes look at her kindly.

"I guess you're not much of a drinker," he says.

Stephie blushes. "You're right."

Bengt extends a hand and pats her cheek. "Did you ever see a prettier face?" he asks Rikard and Vera.

Stephie sips her drink as the others finish the contents of the pocket flask and move on to another bottle Rikard got from inside the house. They all talk and laugh. Although she hasn't had much to drink, Stephie is dizzy. It's all so new to her. New and exciting. The moonlight. The scents. Bengt's gray eyes searching hers.

She barely notices when Vera and Rikard get up and disappear into the cabin.

"Stephanie," Bengt says, reaching out again. "Won't you come sit next to me?"

He's on a settee, she's in an armchair. The spots

69

where Rikard and Vera were sitting a little while ago are empty now.

"Come on," Bengt repeats. "Sit over here."

Stephie moves to the couch. Bengt puts his arm around her. She leans her head on his shoulder. It feels good. She's so tired.

A little while later, he tilts her face toward his and kisses her.

Stephie's been kissed once before. By Sven, that time he said she was like a younger sister to him. She had made him kiss her then, and not like a brother kisses a sister, but for real, on the lips.

But this kiss is different. Bengt presses his lips to hers, hard.

"Come on, open up," he mumbles.

She opens her lips. His tongue pushes inside them, between her top and bottom teeth, seeking hers. It feels awful and nice at the same time. Her whole body is tingling in a way she's never felt before.

"My little Jewess," Bengt whispers.

His hand is on her left breast. What if he feels the stocking bundled in her bra! What if it falls out?

Now his hand is sliding down her body. He kisses her again. His hand reaches under her skirt, up her leg, toward the edge of her garter. . . .

This is wrong. She doesn't want him doing this. She tries to break free, but he holds her tight. Now his hand is on the inside of her thigh, between her stocking and her underwear.

"Stop!" she cries.

His face moves a few inches from hers. His eyes don't look as kind as before.

"What's your problem?" he asks, annoyed.

"Let me go!" she says, pushing at his hand.

Bengt glowers at her. "Don't play innocent," he says. "A girl who goes off with guys like you did tonight can't refuse. What do you imagine Rikard and your girlfriend are up to?"

Stephie listens. From inside the cabin, she hears a rhythmic creaking from the springs of a bed or a couch.

"I didn't know," she says. "Leave me alone."

She puts the palms of both hands to his chest and pushes him away.

Bengt lets go, and she is freed.

"Is it me you don't like?" he asks, sounding glum.

"No!" she is quick to reply.

"There must be something wrong with me," Bengt insists. "Don't try to make me believe you're a virgin. I've heard a thing or two . . ."

"What have you heard?"

". . . about Jewish girls," says Bengt. "They say you're the hottest girls in town. That's what I've heard."

Stephie just stares at him. She can hardly believe she saw anything handsome or kind in his gray eyes. Now she finds them ugly, bleary with drink, and scary in some other way, too. She gets up.

"I'm leaving," she says.

He doesn't answer her. Just slouches on the settee,

watching her put on her coat. She hears Vera giggle in the cabin. *How can she?*

Stephie stumbles down the porch steps. The singing from the other cabin sounds more like drunken bellowing now. But above it she hears Bengt's voice, saying awful words.

"Just go, then!" he shouts. "Go to hell, you little Jewish slut."

She practically runs down the path through the woods. The moon has gone behind a cloud, and it's hard to see her way. The bushes rustle and a big bird rises. She wishes she could turn around and run back to the brightly lit porch. But Bengt is there. She never wants to see him again. Never!

Stephie stumbles, breaking one of the heels on her borrowed pumps. She takes them off and continues in her stocking feet, paying no heed to the fact that she is still wearing Vera's silk stockings. She's sure to have ruined them already. What does she care, though? This whole thing is Vera's fault. She ought to have known better. She's used to being around boys.

Stephie finally reaches the country road. There are no buses at this hour, of course. She pulls off the torn silk stockings and starts walking barefoot in the direction of town. After a while, she gets a lift with a truck driver. He's a nice man and asks her no questions. He drops her at Järntorget, in the middle of town.

It's beginning to get light out, and the trams have

started running. Stephie reaches Sandarna at half past five. She unlocks the door quietly and sneaks inside. Luckily, May's parents don't hear her, but May wakes up when Stephie gets into bed. Stephie tries to give her a smile, a smile that says everything's all right.

Though nothing is really all right. Nothing at all.

12

Stephie dozes uneasily for a couple of hours. The sheets tangle around her, trapping her arms and legs.

She dreams someone's trying to catch her. Hands reach out, touching her body. She's got a tingling sensation in the palms of her hands, on her lips, between her legs.

"Stephanie," a voice says. "Stephanie, Stephanie!"

The voice resembles Sven's. She turns around fast, and finds herself looking into a pair of gray eyes. But the eyes aren't Sven's, they're Bengt's, and the expression on his face is cold and scornful.

When she wakes up, she feels dirty. She spends a long time in the bathroom, washing her body from head to toe.

She tells May she went to Vera's to spend the night,

but they sat up talking until dawn, so she decided to head home.

"What was it like?" asks May. "Did you get to dance much?"

"Quite a lot," Stephie tells her. "But not as much as Vera."

She tells her what it looked like at Rota and what she and Vera wore. But when May asks about the boys she danced with, Stephie answers curtly.

"One with glasses. And another one called Bengt."

~

Not until one-thirty, just as she's about to leave for Miss Björk's, does Stephie realize her own clothes are still at Vera's. And her shoes, what about her shoes? They are her only spring pair. She has to put on her heavy winter boots in spite of the warm weather.

"Good luck!" May wishes her. "I hope Miss Björk's thought of something."

Half an hour later, Stephie arrives at Hedvig Björk's apartment and rings the doorbell. When she is let in, she hangs up her coat and leaves her boots in the tiny hall before following Miss Björk into her combined bedroom, study, and living room.

Stephie has always liked this apartment. The walls have floor-to-ceiling bookshelves. In front of the large window are a desk and a good chair. The bed in the corner is hidden during the day by a pretty curtain with calming colors—burgundy, gray-blue, and a pleasant shade of yellow. A comfortable armchair for reading sits in front of the fireplace, and next to it is a little table holding a pile of books.

Miss Björk moves the books aside and pulls the desk chair over to the table. While she's in the kitchen getting the tea tray, Stephie examines the photographs on the mantelpiece. There's a cute picture of Hedvig Björk as a child, and several of her parents and relatives.

Stephie notices a new picture, one that wasn't here two years ago when Stephie was staying with Miss Björk. A woman in her thirties is looking solemnly into the camera. Could this be a sister? No, Stephie's teacher has never mentioned brothers and sisters, and the woman in the picture doesn't look at all like her. The woman's mouth is softer, her nose pointier, and her face is surrounded by a mound of frizzy hair.

Miss Björk sets down the tray, which holds a teapot, two cups, and some slices of bread with butter and cucumber.

"English sandwiches," she explains with a smile. "You sit in the armchair. I spent the morning there."

She serves the tea and sips hers thoughtfully. Stephie is all pins and needles.

"I'm assuming you really want to continue on to high school," Miss Björk finally says.

"Very much."

"And that you're prepared to make some sacrifices to do so?"

Sacrifices? Stephie doesn't really understand, but she answers, "Yes."

"In that case, I have a proposal," says Miss Björk. "I've had a word with the headmaster, and he believes, as I do, that your grades and sharp mind are strong enough for you to skip the first year altogether. That would mean you'd only have two years to go, just one more than for the junior secondary diploma. We might be able to get the relief committee to accept that as a compromise. Of course, you'll have to do the first-year courses on your own over the summer and take an entrance exam to the second year before the fall term begins. It won't be easy, but I have an idea how to solve that, too. I'll tell you in a few minutes. What do you think?"

"Miss Björk, are you sure I can manage it?"

"If I weren't, I wouldn't suggest it. There's one further condition, though."

"What is it?"

"That you call the relief committee yourself and put the proposal to them. It's your future that's on the line. You're old enough to take on the responsibility."

Stephie nods.

"And now for my second idea," Miss Björk continues. "Since you'd be studying a whole year's worth of coursework over the summer, I think you'd need help. Do you know whether your foster parents have already rented their rooms to summer guests?"

"I don't believe so."

"In that case, would you ask them if a woman friend of mine and I could be your summer tenants this year?" Miss Björk asks. "I'll work on the math and science courses with you for a couple of hours every day. My friend's from England, so she'll give you English lessons. She's the woman in that photo, by the way. Her name is Janice. You're going to like her. You already speak German, so that's not a problem, and I'll get you a reading list."

"But don't you want the summer off if you're going to spend it on the island?"

Miss Björk smiles. "Summer days are long," she says. "And you're the one who'll have to do most of the work. You won't have much of a vacation, of course. Any second thoughts?"

"None."

"Well, then why don't you call the relief committee right now? I'll go out to the kitchen so you can have some privacy."

Stephie sits down at the desk, and Miss Björk leaves the room, shutting the door behind her. Stephie has to start by calling Aunt Märta to ask for the number of her official guardian on the relief committee.

"You're not going to call and nag, are you? I don't think it's any use," Aunt Märta says.

"Miss Björk has an idea," Stephie tells her. "If it works out, I'll tell you all about it."

She takes the opportunity to ask Aunt Märta if she already has tenants lined up for the summer. She doesn't.

"Miss Björk and a woman friend of hers would like to rent," says Stephie. "For the whole summer."

"I'll give her a good price in that case," says Aunt Märta. "Ask her to phone me, and I'm sure we can work it out. Incidentally, did you hear they found the *Wolf*?"

No, Stephie hadn't heard.

"On Tuesday," Aunt Märta tells her. "A fishing boat from the island of Hälso thought their nets were stuck on the seabed, but it was the *Wolf*. The navy brought in divers. They said a mine had done it in. Everyone on board was dead. It was awful. Young fellows, most of them."

After their conversation, Stephie sits there for a few minutes, receiver in hand. Her mouth is dry. She gets her cup and takes a swallow of cold tea. Then she calls the number she'd jotted down.

She knows the lady on the other end is the one who accompanied her and Nellie from the railroad station to the boat when they first came to Sweden. But she hasn't seen her since. She can't remember what she looks like, only that she was wearing a yellow suit.

"Hello," Stephie says. "Stephanie Steiner speaking."

"Stephanie," the lady says. "How are you?"

"I'm sorry to trouble you," Stephie says, "on a Sunday and all. . . ."

"Yes?"

She has to pull herself together. Tell the woman why she's calling. Like a grown-up.

"It's about my education," she goes on. "High school. I want to continue very badly."

"I see," the lady says. "But as I've already told Mrs. Jansson, we cannot afford to put every child through upper secondary school. You must realize you're not the only one who wants further schooling."

"But you said yes to one year?"

"As I told Mrs. Jansson."

"What about two?"

"Two?"

"My homeroom teacher has offered to help me through the first year over the summer," Stephie explains. "So I can finish high school in two years."

There is silence at the other end of the line.

"An interesting proposal. Let me think about it," the lady says. "I cannot make such a decision on my own. What's your homeroom teacher's name?"

"Hedvig Björk."

The lady asks for Miss Björk's telephone number, and Stephie gives it to her. She promises to have an answer for Stephie within a week. They agree that she will inform Miss Björk of the committee's decision since there is no telephone where Stephie lives. Stephie says thank you and hangs up.

"I did it," she rejoices to herself. "I did it!"

Hedvig Björk and Stephie take a walk along the streets in the neighborhood, which are empty on a Sunday afternoon. Then Miss Björk accompanies Stephie through the park with the lily pond and down the steps to the tram stop at the crossroads. She waits with Stephie until her tram comes.

"It's all going to work out. I'm confident," she says, giving Stephie a quick kiss on the cheek before leaving.

The tram is almost full, but Stephie spots a seat behind two girls, one her own age, the other a couple of years younger. There's something familiar about the older girl's face, but Stephie can't place her. She doesn't know her from grammar school, anyway. Her hair is curly and strawberry blond, her eyes are blue, and her skin pale and freckled. In spite of being fair-haired and blue-eyed, though, she doesn't look Swedish.

As soon as Stephie sits down, the girl with the curly hair turns around.

"Stephanie Steiner?" she asks in German. "Aren't you Stephanie Steiner from Vienna?"

13

The memory flashes through Stephie's mind like a bolt of lightning. Of course she knows the girl! They were in the same class at the Jewish school in Vienna for several months. The crowded classroom with far too many pupils. The hunger. The fear.

"Yes, indeed," Stephie says. "I'm Stephie Steiner. And you're Judith Liebermann."

Judith nods. "I didn't know you were in Göteborg, too," she says. "How long have you been in Sweden?"

"Since August 1939. What about you?" Stephie asks.

"April."

Right. Stephie remembers Judith leaving the class sometime that spring. Nobody paid much attention. Children came and went at the Jewish school. People suddenly got emigration permits. But Judith's family was one of the ones with the least chance of getting out to the West. Polish Jews, lots of children, no money.

"Where are you living?" asks Judith.

Stephie tells her. "And you?"

"I'm at the Jewish Children's Home," Judith says. "This is Susie. She lives there, too."

Stephie didn't even know there *was* a Jewish Children's Home in Göteborg. Judith tells her about it. It is girls only, mostly teenagers, a few younger.

"I started out with a Jewish family," says Judith. "Since my parents are orthodox, Papa absolutely insisted I live with other Jews. It hardly mattered, though, as the family wasn't at all religious. They never went to synagogue. They found me difficult, and after six months, they didn't want me anymore. I was sent to a farm in Dalsland, where they made me eat pork and tend to the pigs in the barn. In the end, I cried day and night, so they didn't want me, either. Then I was with a Swedish family in Borås, where I was more or less their housemaid. Still, they were the best family because they let me be. But last fall, they moved to Stockholm, and I ended up at the Children's Home."

"What a lot of bad luck you've had," Stephie says sympathetically.

"Oh, I don't know about that! Susie here was at five

different places before she ended up at the Children's Home last winter," Judith tells her.

Stephie looks at Susie, a girl with a sturdy build, frowning face, and sad eyes.

"This is our stop," says Judith. She gets up and touches Stephie's arm. "Come with us for a while. Unless you're in a hurry?"

Stephie thinks for a second. It will soon be dinnertime at May's, but she's still full from Miss Björk's English sandwiches. Besides, with ten people at the Karlssons' table, one more body or less doesn't really make any difference.

"No," she says. "I'm not in a hurry."

They get off the tram.

"Are they stingy?" Susie asks. "The family you live with."

"What do you mean?"

Susie points to Stephie's feet. "You've got your boots on still, and it's May."

Though she doesn't want to explain what happened to her shoes, Stephie doesn't want Susie and Judith to get the wrong idea about Aunt Märta and Uncle Evert.

"My spring shoes are at the shoemaker's, being resoled," she fibs.

They walk up a little hill with ornamented wooden houses on both sides of the street. One of them is the Children's Home.

Judith shows her around the home and introduces

her to the girls who are there. Several of them are from Vienna, and Stephie recognizes a few. One girl even arrived in Göteborg on the same train as Stephie and Nellie.

"I had no idea there were so many of us," she says to Judith.

"I think there are about five hundred," Judith tells her, "all over Sweden."

"Five hundred!"

Judith looks at her coolly. "That's not so many," she says. "Just remember how many got left behind! And Sweden's happy to receive Finnish children as refugees. Tens of thousands of them. They're blond and blue-eyed and fit right in with the Swedes."

"You're blond and blue-eyed yourself," Stephie reminds her.

"Yes, but I'm Jewish. You know what I mean."

They're sitting in the girls' dayroom. The house is full of noisy voices, footsteps on the stairs, kitchen clatter.

"How about your family?" Judith asks. "Do you know where they are?"

"My parents are in Theresienstadt. My little sister's here."

Judith doesn't say anything for a while.

"You're lucky to have someone in your family here," she finally goes on. "And there are worse places than Theresienstadt."

"Where's your family?"

"Two of my brothers are in Palestine," Judith tells her. "They left before me, in 1938. My sister wanted to go along, but Papa thought she was too young. By the time I got sent here, she was too old to come with me."

"Too old?"

"You have to be under sixteen to be considered a child refugee," Judith explains. "Edith had turned seventeen. You don't seem to know much about all this."

"Where are they now?"

"My oldest brother was shot," says Judith. "Three years ago. Mamma, Papa, and Edith were deported to Poland in 1941. At first I got a few letters, but I haven't heard from them for a year and a half now."

"Do you think they're . . ." Stephie hesitates.

"I don't know. You hear terrible things about Poland. Death camps . . . and gas."

"Gas?"

"Theresienstadt's better," says Judith. "You should be glad your parents are there."

They sit quietly. The house is full of sounds that seem both close and yet far away. Outside an open window, the fresh spring leaves of a large chestnut tree rustle in the wind.

"Susie has two younger brothers," Judith says suddenly. "She was nine when she came from Berlin. Her brothers were two and five, and Susie's mother thought they were too small to make the trip."

"Where are they now?"

"Susie doesn't know. She stopped getting letters six months ago."

"How awful!"

Stephie feels ashamed. Because she knows so much less than Judith, because she gets cards from her parents, and because she isn't actually all alone.

"When the war's over, I'll go to Palestine and join my brothers," Judith tells her. "I want to take part in building up a country of our own. A country for all the Jews, where no one can persecute us."

Stephie doesn't know much about Palestine. She has a vague picture of a desert, the ocean, and burning sunshine. Somewhere far away.

"Yes," she says slowly. "That sounds good."

"I'm saving up for the journey," Judith tells her. "I save every bit of money that's left after my expenses here. That's why I stay on at the Children's Home. It's cheaper than renting a room."

"Where do you work?"

"At the chocolate factory. I never thought I could hate the smell of chocolate."

Stephie bites her lip. She feels spoiled asking for even more money for her studies, while Judith slaves away at a factory.

"Come see us again," Judith says when Stephie leaves. "You must be lonely, surrounded by nothing but Swedes. Though you do have your sister. But we're your own people. We're of a kind. Come whenever you like."

Of a kind. Those words echo in Stephie's head along with the rhythm of the tram on the tracks taking her home to Sandarna.

Of a kind.

fried herring. It's dinnertime. Two flights up, they stop in front of a door bearing a handwritten sign: *Irja Andersson*.

Stephie steps into Irja's kitchen. There's a laundry line running straight across the whole room, full of underwear. Flesh-colored underpants, a bra, and a slip.

"Sorry." Irja gestures at her laundry. "Yesterday was my day off, so I did laundry. Have a seat."

Stephie sits at the kitchen table. Irja takes the coffeepot and makes and pours two cups.

"I don't have any sugar," Irja says. "Do you mind?"

"No," says Stephie. "That's all right. Thanks."

Stephie takes a swallow of the bitter coffee. She's got to say something. Irja must wonder why she came.

But before Stephie can figure out how to start, Irja smiles kindly at her.

"Nice of you to come by," she says. "Sven used to talk about you a lot."

Used to. Apparently he's forgotten her now.

Irja drinks from her cup. Something gleams on her left-hand ring ringer.

An engagement ring.

They're engaged. Irja and Sven.

"Congratulations," Stephie says, a huge lump in her throat.

"Thanks," says Irja.

"When are you getting married?"

"I don't know," says Irja. "With the war on, it's not

14

Stephie feels a strange discomfort in her body, a throbbing heat she doesn't recognize. She doesn't want to think about Bengt and that porch, but she can't get it out of her mind. What happened between the two of them was wrong and she wished she could undo it. But what if it had been a different boy? What if it had been Sven?

Sven. She doesn't think about him very often anymore. But now and then, the memory of him gives her a twinge, like an old wound that has healed but left a scar that pulls.

They saw each other a few times the spring after Stephie moved out of his parents' apartment. They would go to a café and talk about school, about books and music. But they didn't talk about what had happened between them. Sven avoided mentioning Irja, but Stephie knew they were still seeing each other.

She didn't attend the party his family held to celebrate his graduation, in spite of his invitation, and in spite of the fact that she knew Irja wasn't coming. When autumn came, Sven went off to the university in Lund to study literature. Now he is doing his military service somewhere near the Norwegian border. She hasn't heard from him since last winter when he sent her a New Year's card. She doesn't have his address.

Stephie doesn't decide to get off the tram at Kaptensgatan. She just does. She doesn't know why she's there, but her feet know where they're going as they lead her out the tram door.

She stops in front of the tavern where Irja works, and where Sven used to pay her sneak visits.

Through the window, she sees the drab brown interior and the old men sitting there with their beers. Girls like her don't go to such places. What if the old men are rude to her?

A girl comes out from the kitchen, carrying a tray of bottles and glasses. She's not Irja.

Stephie is about to leave. But then she realizes that even if Irja doesn't work there anymore, the new girl may know where she's gone.

Gathering her courage, she opens the door. Everyone seems to be staring at her.

"Hello, sweetie," says one of the old men. "Can I buy you a beer? Or are you lost?"

Stephie looks at him in horror. But the eyes in his unshaven face are kind and heavy. He's only teasing.

"Excuse me," she says to the waitress. "I'm looking for Irja. Does she still work here?"

"Sure she does," the waitress answers.

She turns toward the curtain separating the tavern from the kitchen.

"Irja, you've got a visitor!" she shouts.

Stephie wants to turn and run. Take off out the door, rush back down Kaptensgatan to the tram stop. What did she come in here for, anyway? What is she going to say to Irja?

But her feet stay rooted to the ground.

The curtain is swept aside.

Irja is standing there. She looks bewildered.

"Who . . . ?"

Stephie's throat constricts and she can't get out single word.

Irja inspects her closely. "Oh, aren't you . . . ?" she says slowly. "Aren't you Stephanie?"

"That's right," Stephie whispers.

Irja's face lights up. "Well, then come on home with me. I've just finished for today!"

Irja lives on a street that crosses Kaptensgatan, just two blocks away. The stairwell smells of cabbage and

the best time to get married and start a family. I guess we'll wait a while." She takes another sip from her cup. "Actually, we haven't been a couple very long. We need time to get to know each other."

What does she mean by that? Sven and Irja have known each other for at least two and a half years.

"Oh?" says Stephie.

Irja can clearly hear her confusion, and laughs. "It's not Sven, if that's what you thought. We split up ages ago."

Stephie can't believe her ears. She remembers Sven saying, "I love Irja. We love each other."

How can that kind of love—when two people love each other—be over?

"It could never have worked out between the two of us," Irja goes on. "You know, he didn't even dare tell his parents about me."

"He would have," says Stephie. "He was planning to tell them. I know he was."

Irja smiles. "There's no need to stand up for him," she says. "It's all over now. We were too different." Her blue eyes are clear and musing. "I'm surprised you didn't know. Don't you two write to each other?"

"No," Stephie mumbles. "No, we've lost touch."

"My fiancé's name is Jon," Irja tells her. "He's a refugee from Norway."

They talk about the war for a few minutes.

"They know what side their bread is buttered on, the

Swedish government. As long as it looked as if the Germans were going to win, the whole government bowed down to the Germans. But now that everybody knows the Allies are going to come out on top, they're singing a different tune. They'll manage to stay on the right side."

After some time, Irja looks at the clock and tells Stephie that Jon will be coming any minute. Stephie realizes she ought to leave. Thanking Irja for the coffee, she gets up to go. Irja walks her to the door and extends a hand. They shake solemnly, like two grown-ups.

"Good-bye," says Irja.

"Good-bye."

15

Wednesday morning, Miss Björk finds Stephie in the hall. She doesn't have to say a word. Her smiling face tells Stephie everything she needs to know.

"They said yes," Miss Björk says anyway, giving Stephie a hug. "They said yes! I just wanted to tell you right away. We'll talk more later."

In spite of her joy, Stephie can feel some of the other girls in the class giving her unkind looks. She knows some of them think she and Miss Björk are too close. That Stephie's a teacher's pet. That Stephie gets better grades than she deserves in Miss Björk's classes.

Miss Björk asks Stephie to drop by the staff room at lunchtime. She tells her the relief committee has agreed to pay her expenses for two more years, though a lower sum per year.

"It will cover your room and board," she says, "but you'll have to earn your own pocket money, I'm afraid. If you like, I can try to find you someone to tutor next fall. I'm sure you could give some junior secondary girls private lessons in math—and why not German as well?" She gives Stephie a proud smile. "I'm so happy for you," she says. "And I'm glad we'll be spending the summer together, too."

"Aren't you meeting Vera tonight?" May asks her after they've had dinner, done the dishes, and finished their homework. "It's Wednesday."

"No" is all Stephie says.

May looks as if she expects an explanation, but when none is forthcoming, she changes the subject.

After May leaves for her youth group meeting, Stephie collects what's left of her outfit from the previous Saturday. Vera's dress and bra, the torn silk stockings, and the pumps that have lost a heel. She finds some brown paper and makes a parcel.

Tomorrow, when Vera has her afternoon off, she plans to take the things with her to school. After school, she'll ring the doorbell of Vera's employers and say she has a package for Vera. If there's no one home, she'll just hang the package on the door handle.

The problem is getting her own things back. She needs them, especially the shoes. She's been walking around in boots for four days now. They're hot and heavy, and she notices people staring.

She doesn't know how she's ever going to get them.

♆

Stephie doesn't have to ring Vera's doorbell after all. As she's leaving school the next day, she notices Vera's head of red hair outside the gate. She's standing there with a brown paper parcel almost identical to the one Stephie is carrying.

"Stephie!" she calls, waving.

Stephie walks over to her, feeling stiff and awkward.

"You never came to the café last night," Vera says reproachfully. "I waited for hours."

Stephie's anger boils up inside. "Did you really expect me to come?" she hisses. "After what happened on Saturday? Here, take your things. The stockings are ruined. The shoes, too."

She presses her package into Vera's arms, grabbing her own belongings.

Vera looks embarrassed. "I'm really sorry," she says. "I hope you know I didn't plan for that to happen. Come on, won't you just listen to me a little? Please?"

"No," Stephie says.

"Please," Vera repeats. "Stephie? Don't do this to me. You're . . . you're my only real friend."

Stephie looks at Vera. Her green eyes are brimming with tears.

"All right, then. But I only have a little while."

They walk to the lily pond. Stephie thinks they must look quite strange. Two girls, each with a brown paper parcel in her arms.

"I never thought . . . that Bengt . . . Well, he's always been so polite and well behaved. I thought the two of you would sit out on the porch and flirt, maybe share a kiss or two. Or take a walk in the moonlight. I really never imagined he'd go after you like that."

"He told me girls who go off with boys late at night only have themselves to blame," Stephie says, her voice raspy, as if she can hardly get the words out.

Vera sighs. "He must be more of an idiot than I realized."

"And what about you?"

Vera stands stock-still. "What do you mean by that?"

"Don't you think we could hear what you and Rikard were doing inside?"

"Stephie," says Vera, "I . . ."

"Is that what you always do? Jump right into bed with whatever boy you meet out dancing?"

"What kind of girl do you think I am?" Vera asks indignantly. "Of course not. That was the first time."

Stephie is confused. There's something she doesn't understand. Something's not right.

"Are you in love with Rikard?"

"Of course I am," Vera replies.

She looks at Stephie. Her green eyes are pleading. "Don't you believe me? Stephie?"

It's impossible to be mad at Vera. As with so many times before, Stephie's anger vanishes like smoke. Putting her parcel under her right arm, she takes Vera's left arm in hers.

"Sorry about your stockings," she says.

"That's all right," says Vera. "Rota's going to be closing for the season soon, and there won't be any more dancing for a while."

"Well, you can count on one thing," Stephie adds. "I'm never going there with you again."

⁓

On the doormat at May's, Stephie finds a card waiting for her.

Theresienstadt, 10 April 1943

Stephie!

Tonight Mamma was supposed to sing Queen of the Night. But yesterday they banned all culture.

We're well and thinking, as always, of you and Nellie.

Papa

A few words in the middle of the card have been crossed out in heavy black ink—not the blue ink of Papa's pen. Someone else must have crossed them out. *Why?* Stephie wonders. What did he write that Stephie isn't supposed to read? Only thirty words and somebody's stolen three of them. Those words were hers and Papa's.

Because she's so angry about the stolen words, it takes her a while to absorb the rest of the text. When she does, she feels even angrier, and sad, too. Poor Mamma. She'd been so looking forward to singing Queen of the Night. How disappointed she must have been.

Someone Stephie has never met and whose face she has never seen wields power over Mamma and Papa. He can keep Mamma from singing and Papa from writing whatever he wants to. He wields power over Stephie, too, since her life is connected to theirs.

She hates that nameless, faceless man she'll never meet.

If only the war would end!

16

On Saturday evening, Stephie and May take a blanket, a thermos of coffee, and a few sweet rolls outside. Britten watches them longingly, but they don't invite her to come along. They want to be alone to talk.

They go up to the top of the hill, where Sandarna is situated and find a crevice in the cliffside to keep them out of the wind. They spread out the blanket. Behind them are the frames of what will be more new apartment buildings. The streets up there are all named after the islands in the archipelago. There's one with the name of Stephie's island.

The river gleams in the evening sun. Below the steep slope, they can see the sheds and warehouses in the harbor. On the other side of the river are cranes and docks at the shipyard where May's father works. Seagulls and terns circle overhead. Near where they are sitting, a sloe bush is in bloom, a sea of creamy white blossoms.

May removes the cork from the thermos and pours two mugs of coffee.

"It's a beautiful evening," she says.

"Mmm," Stephie agrees.

"Want a roll?"

"Yes, please."

"Stephie?"

"What?"

"You don't have to tell me if you don't want to, but if there's something on your mind . . . you know I'd never say a peep to anybody."

May's eyes look serious and steady. Yes, Stephie knows she can trust May.

"Last Saturday wasn't much fun," she begins. "At first, hardly anyone asked me to dance. Then Vera brought over two boys she knew. One of them was called Bengt."

Telling the story makes her feel so foolish. Falling for a pair of gray eyes and a strong arm. But May doesn't laugh; she just listens quietly.

Now Stephie's telling about the porch. The settee. Bengt's hands on her.

"But where was Vera?" asks May. "And that other boy?"

The creaking from inside the cabin. She can't tell May about that.

"They'd gone for a walk," Stephie fibs. "In the moon-light."

"So what did you do?"

"I ran away."

She doesn't tell May about what Bengt shouted after her, either. It hurts too much to say aloud.

"You did the right thing," May tells her, her eyes welling up with tears behind her glasses. Stephie wonders whether anyone has ever tried to kiss May.

⁊

A couple of days later, the next card arrives. This one is from Mamma.

Theresienstadt, 14 April 1943

Dearest!

Your long letter made me very happy. But why doesn't Nellie write? She's not sick, is she? We haven't heard from her for several months.

Thousands of kisses from
Your Mamma

I write once a week.

That was what Nellie said. But she was lying.

Doesn't she realize how worried Mamma and Papa must be when they don't hear from her? Doesn't she understand how important the girls' letters are to them?

She's got to talk to Nellie. She needs to do it right

away. This can't wait until the semester is over, though Stephie hadn't planned to go back to the island until then. She'll go on Sunday.

≈

Stephie takes an early-morning boat on Sunday. It's only eight o'clock, but she can feel in the air that it's going to be a hot day. The boat is full of noisy young people and families with picnic baskets, on their way to a day's outing on one of the islands.

Today there is no bicycle leaning against the boathouse. Stephie makes the long walk across the island, with only the ringing church bells to keep her company.

At the house, she finds Aunt Märta in her Sunday dress, sitting in the rocker and reading the Bible.

"Stephie? Today? What a surprise!"

Stephie doesn't explain why she's there. That's between her and Nellie.

She rides her bike over to Auntie Alma's that afternoon. Nellie, Elsa, and John have just returned from Sunday school. They're sitting in the garden with Auntie Alma, drinking berry juice.

"Nellie," says Stephie. "I need to talk to you."

"What is it now?" Nellie asks grumpily.

"Come on," say Stephie. "Let's take a walk."

"I don't feel like it," says Nellie. "We just got home."

Stephie doesn't know what to say. She wants to talk

to Nellie alone. But if she starts out upset, she'll never get her to listen.

"Nellie," says Auntie Alma in a gentle tone of voice. "You go with Stephie now. She may have something important to tell you."

Nellie gets up reluctantly. They walk in the direction of the little beach.

"You know Mamma and Papa are in a camp, right?" Stephie begins. "We don't know very much about what life is like there, but I'm sure it's very difficult."

"I know that," Nellie says impatiently. "You've told me a hundred times."

"I imagine Mamma and Papa worry a lot," Stephie goes on. "Papa worries about Mamma, I know that.

"Yeah, yeah."

"Don't you think the least the two of us can do is not to worry them even more?"

"What do you mean by that?"

Stephie takes out Mamma's card from her dress pocket and shows it to Nellie. Nellie reads it and hands it back. She stares stubbornly at the ground.

"Well?"

"I do write," says Nellie. "Sometimes."

"Nellie," says Stephie, "don't you see?"

Nellie looks up at her, her eyes flaming. "They sent us away!" she shouts. "They didn't want us. Why should I care about them?"

Nellie's words threaten to drown Stephie. If feels like

when she's at the beach and a big wave throws her off balance in the water. She can't see; she can't hear; all she can taste is salt. Stephie struggles for a foothold.

She can't get an answer out. Can't explain what they both know. Mamma and Papa sent them away to keep them safe. All she wants to do is cry, cry as she did so long ago, their first evening on the island. *Mamma, come and get me. Come and get me or I'll die.*

But at the very moment the wave of grief threatens to overwhelm her, it turns into coal-hot anger. She slaps Nellie—slaps her so hard, her sister shouts out in pain.

By the time Stephie has pulled herself together, Nellie is gone. She's running up the path to the village, her long black braids flapping behind her back.

"Nellie!" Stephie calls out.

But Nellie doesn't turn around.

❧

The palm of Stephie's hand is burning. Her cheeks are burning, too, as if she were the one who was slapped. She has only been slapped once in her life, and that was by Aunt Märta, the time she came home with a rip in her dress.

Mamma and Papa never hit them.

How could that have happened? How could she have slapped Nellie?

17

Stephie writes another long letter to Mamma. She says Nellie has actually written several times, but the letters must have gotten lost in the mail. *Maybe she wrote the address wrong,* she lies. *Or forgot the stamp. If the letters are returned, we'll send them again.*

She hates lying to Mamma. But she can't tell the truth. It's too awful. Just like that very first letter she wrote to Mamma and Papa back in Vienna, when she and Nellie had just arrived on the island, the letter she never sent. The truth is that she has been lying to them ever since she got to Sweden. Perhaps not as blatantly as now; now she has invented pure falsehoods to cover up Nellie's refusal to write. But she has been altering the truth, exaggerating the good things and keeping silent about the difficulties and sorrows.

She begins to wonder what Mamma and Papa think of her. Do they imagine that she is as happy as she sounds, or can they see through her words? They certainly ought to know her better. But it's been nearly four years. When she left, she was a twelve-year-old child. Now she's nearly sixteen.

Another thought comes to mind: What if Mamma and Papa are doing the same thing? What if they're not telling her the whole truth? What if they don't want to upset her? What if that nameless German doesn't let them tell the truth? What if everything is much worse than she thinks?

By the time Stephie seals the letter, she has a painful lump in her throat. She mails the envelope on her way to school.

Two weeks later the letter comes back.

&

"What was stamped on it?" Judith asks. "Did it say *Adressat abgereist*?"

"No," says Stephie. "Just *Return to Sender*."

"That's all right, then," says Judith. "Your mother may have moved to a different barracks. Or there may have been some mistake with the mail. I can't say for certain. But I'm sure your next letter will reach her."

Abgereist? Stephie wonders. *Departed? What did Judith mean? Where would Mamma have gone?*

Judith presses her lips together and refuses to say any more about it.

The two girls are taking a walk; it's a lovely early summer evening. The lindens in the lane are in pale green bloom, and the flowers on the chestnut trees shine like white candles. They walk down to the moat that circles the old town. They sit on the edge, dangling their feet.

"I see you've picked up your spring shoes from the shoemaker," Judith says, looking at Stephie's feet.

"I have."

"I actually thought you were lying about them," Judith tells her. "You gave me such a funny look when you told me they were being resoled. What are your foster parents like, really?"

Stephie does her best to describe Aunt Märta and Uncle Evert. Judith listens attentively.

"Swedish people are so strange," she says when Stephie is done. "You'd think they were as thick-skinned as elephants and had no feelings."

"Oh, they do have feelings," says Stephie. "Only they show them differently."

"I just wish the war would end and I could go to Palestine," Judith says. "Where will you go?"

"Home, I imagine," says Stephie.

"Home?" Judith asks. "We don't have homes anymore. They took away our homes. They took away our right to live."

"But after the war," says Stephie, "when the Germans are gone, don't you think things can be like they were before?"

"Things will never be like before. Never!"

Stephie considers. Judith may be right.

"We lived in Leopoldstadt," says Judith. "I'll never forget when they blew up the synagogue on Leopoldsgasse. Huge blocks of stone flew yards and yards up into the air. It looked like a war zone."

Judith lies down on the grassy edge of the canal, her legs extended straight out over the dark surface of the water. She clasps her hands behind her head and stares up into the sky.

"I hope it will all be gone," she says. "Every single house, every single church, every single street. I hope they bomb it all to rack and ruin. All of Vienna. I hope no one will be able to make a home there again. Never ever."

Stephie looks down at Judith's lovely face surrounded by her curly angelic head of hair. Her blue eyes gleam with hate.

She tries to imagine Vienna leveled to the ground. Her school in ruins, the house where they lived crushed by a bomb. The beautiful streets with the shop windows black gaping holes, the tram tracks torn up. The big Ferris wheel in Prater Park a distorted steel skeleton.

"No," says Stephie. "I wouldn't want that."

Then she sees that Judith is crying.

❧

Stephie is unable to get Judith's words out of her mind. *We don't have homes anymore.*

Until now, she always imagined that when the war was over, things would be like before. That Mamma, Papa, Nellie, and she would return to their big apartment near Prater Park and that they would be a family again.

But other people live in their apartment now, people who aren't Jewish and therefore have the right to live normal lives. Unless the house has been bombed, as Judith wishes.

And can they ever be a family again? Is it possible to be reunited just like that, after four, five, or six years, and live together as if nothing had happened? If the war goes on for a couple more years, Stephie will be an adult when it ends. Nellie, her little sister, will be an obstinate teenager who feels more at home in Sweden than in Vienna.

The thought of Nellie makes her stomach seize up. They used to be so close. Now they live separate lives. It's as though they're not even sisters.

The memory of slapping Nellie burns Stephie's insides. She doesn't want to think about it.

It will work out, she persuades herself. *We are a family. We love each other. It may take some time, but we will have a good life. If only the war will end.*

We has a different meaning to Stephie and Judith. To Stephie, *we* means "my family." To Judith, it means "all Jews."

Before the Germans came, Stephie never thought of

herself as a Jew. Being Jewish simply meant going to synagogue a few times a year, the same way her Christian friends went to church at Christmas and Easter. It was the Germans who separated her and Nellie, Mamma, and Papa from the others, made them members of a particular group, forced them to move and forced the girls to change schools.

The Germans made her a Jew. When she came to the island, she became a Christian. A member of the Pentecostal church, "redeemed" and baptized. But always filled with secret doubts. With a feeling of not belonging, a feeling of pretending.

Judith seems so sure of who she is. Sometimes Stephie envies her that, even though she knows the war and persecution have caused Judith more problems than they have her. But Judith's *we* is broader and less fragile. And she has brothers in Palestine, as well as her dream of joining them there.

What do I have? Stephie asks herself. *Who am I? Who am I going to become?*

18

After the end-of-semester gathering in the auditorium, Stephie and her classmates go to their homeroom. The atmosphere is solemn. They have been together for three years, and now they are going to be split up. Some will stay at the grammar school for a fourth year and come out with a junior secondary degree. Others will go on to the high school in the same building. A few plan to change schools.

Miss Björk passes out their report cards. She calls each girl up to the front of the room, saying a few personal words to every single one.

"May," she says. "You and math don't get along so well. But after this semester, you'll never have to see each other again. And you'll be able to devote yourself to the things at which you are good. I wish you the very best of luck."

To Harriet, one of the two prettiest and most popular girls in the class, she says, "I get to keep you for another year. You may not be the brightest student, but your sense of humor has lightened up our days. I hope you stay just as you are, not only in school but for your whole life."

Stephie is the second-to-last person on the class roll.

"Stephie," Miss Björk says. "It is a joy for a teacher to have a pupil like you. You have every reason to be satisfied with your grades, and I'm sure when you graduate from high school in two years, your marks will be just as good. We'll see each other again soon!"

As Stephie walks back to her seat, she hears two girls whisper something about her being Miss Björk's pet.

She opens the envelope and looks at her report card. Two B-pluses, otherwise only As and A-minuses. Yes, she is pleased.

&

That evening, Stephie and Vera meet as usual. This will be their last Wednesday at the café for a while. But they will be seeing each other. Vera's employers are going to be the tenants in the summer cottage belonging to the shopkeeper on the island. Vera and her mistress will spend the whole summer there.

"Her heaaaalth's not very good, you know," Vera

tells Stephie, drawing out the word *health* to show how spoiled and affected she thinks her mistress is. "But the fresh sea air and the cold swims will be soooo good for her. And I think her husband's quite glad to be in the city by himself, away from her nagging. He even suggested I stay and do his cooking, but his wife wouldn't hear of it."

Vera tosses her mane of red hair and laughs.

"I'm so glad they're renting on our island and not one of the others," says Stephie. "We'll get to see at least as much of each other as we do here in town. We can go swimming and take bike rides when you have time off. And lie in our special spot on the cliffs, and jump from the rock."

But Vera doesn't look very happy.

"I'd rather be going somewhere else," she says. "See something new. People are such gossips at home."

"What do you mean?"

"Well," Vera says, "actually, if I'd had my choice, I would have stayed in town."

"And done your employer's cooking?"

"No," says Vera. "I wouldn't have stayed alone with him in the apartment. Not on your life."

"Is it because of Rikard that you want to stay in town?"

"Maybe," Vera says, clamming up like a mussel that's been tapped against a stone.

Stephie feels hurt that Vera tells her so little about

Rikard, even though she remembers how she never told Vera or May that she was in love with Sven during her first year at grammar school. That was different, though. It was a secret romance—not even Sven himself knew of her feelings for him.

It's different with Vera and Rikard. They're a couple, which surprises Stephie a little. Vera always said she intended to marry a wealthy man, and Rikard is anything but wealthy. Stephie figures she must be in love with him, although it doesn't always seem that way.

Stephie thinks about how Vera finds the island boring now. It's true that there is nowhere for young people to go out. There are no dance halls, not even outdoor dancing of the kind some of the islands are said to arrange for the summer guests. So it must be dull when you're used to dancing every weekend.

"Well, I'm glad, anyway," says Stephie. "That you're coming to the island, I mean."

When she says that, Vera looks straight into her eyes. Her green gaze is kind.

"I'm sorry," Vera replies. "I'm being silly. Of course it will be fun to spend time with you."

Vera looks down into her coffee cup for a moment. When she looks up again, her expression has changed—as if she had pulled down an invisible visor to shield her from the rest of the world.

"I've got to be going," she says. "See you on the island next week."

The next day, Stephie catches the boat. She's going to help Aunt Märta clean the house for the summer guests, and move their own things down to the basement rooms. At first, Miss Björk insisted that she and her friend could stay in the basement apartment, but Aunt Märta wouldn't hear of it. "Summer guests live up top," she said. "That's how it always is and always will be." Miss Björk had to give in.

It's going to be a summer of hard work. Stephie is going to have to study diligently in order to pass the entrance exam in August. But she'll certainly have some time to relax as well. In July, May will be visiting for a couple of weeks. And her whole family will be coming for a Sunday outing at the beach when the weather is nice.

The boat pulls up to the jetty. Stephie has returned to the island.

19

A week after school lets out, Hedvig Björk and her friend arrive. Stephie and Aunt Märta have spent the whole week taking things down to the basement rooms, airing the bedding, scrubbing the floors, and washing the windows. Now everything is spic-and-span. Stephie has picked wildflowers—saxifrage, cat's-foot, water avens, and forget-me-nots—and put bouquets on the tables in the kitchen and sitting room.

Aunt Märta scoffs at the flowers. "Are you really bringing those weeds inside?"

"Miss Björk is interested in flowers," Stephie tells her. "It's part of her job."

The tenants' suitcases arrive before they do, transported by the shopkeeper's delivery boy on his motorbike. A little while later, the two women come walking down the slope toward the house. Miss Björk has on tight black trousers and a loose shirt. She's most comfortable in trousers, but of course she always wears a skirt at school, or at least culottes.

Her friend Janice has on a flowered summer dress. She is petite and delicate, no bigger than Stephie. In her company, slender Hedvig Björk looks big and strong. Janice has reddish blond hair and a pale, freckled complexion. She has on a wide-brimmed sun hat, probably to protect her skin. When she removes it, Stephie notices that she has green eyes like Vera's.

Aunt Märta has set the table out in the garden, and serves coffee with a freshly baked cake. That cake and the sugar for their coffee has used up the week's whole ration of sugar. But Janice drinks her coffee black and has only half a slice of cake.

Miss Björk and Aunt Märta get along well. They chat as if they were old friends, though they've met just once before.

Janice smiles at Stephie.

"I'm so happy to be here," she says, with a slight English accent. "I've actually never been in the archipelago before, although I've lived in Göteborg since before the war."

Janice is a ballerina, and she has a position at the opera house in Göteborg. That means she performs in ballets and also in some operas that have dancing roles.

Originally, she had planned to be there only a year, but when the war broke out, she ended up having to stay.

Stephie studies Janice. Every move she makes is beautiful. Just the way she lifts her coffee cup to her lips is perfection.

"I can't tell you how much I'm looking forward to this summer," Janice says. "It's lovely here." She waves her arm gently, indicating the sea and the horizon. "I believe people who live by the sea gain wisdom from it," she continues. "From not being shut in like people in the mountains, or tied down to a monotonous plain. Being by the sea gives you an open view. Perhaps that helps people think freely. What do you think?"

"Maybe," says Stephie.

She feels shy in Janice's presence. But she thinks she's going to like her.

Stephie helps Miss Björk carry up their suitcases while Aunt Märta shows Janice the boathouse, the jetty, and the little boat. Miss Björk goes up the stairs first and puts her suitcase in Aunt Märta's and Uncle Evert's bedroom with its double bed. Stephie carries Janice's suitcase into her own little room, setting it beside the bed. She has removed her photographs and other private things. But Jesus still softly smiles down from the painting above the dresser.

The painting was there when Stephie arrived nearly four years ago. She never dared take it down or turn it toward the wall. When she had been baptized and became a member of the Pentecostal congregation, she would look at it for a little while every day, trying to feel the kind of love for Jesus that they talked about at Sunday school. But she never succeeded. She found the painting ugly.

Sven had turned it toward the wall the summer he and his family were summer tenants at Aunt Märta's and Uncle Evert's. But once the family returned to town, the painting was back to its initial position. Elna, Sven's family's housemaid, had turned it face out when they left.

"There was no stopping that woman once she got going," Aunt Märta says to Stephie that evening as they have their dinner in the basement kitchen.

"Who?" Stephie asks, although she thinks she knows who Aunt Märta means.

"The redhead, of course," Aunt Märta replies. "Miss Björk, now, she's a substantial person."

"The redhead's name is Janice," Stephie says with her best English pronunciation.

"Well, she certainly talks a blue streak. Do you know what she asked me? If I had ever spent the night out on one of the skerries! 'Between sea and sky.' What would be the point of that, I ask you?"

"She thinks it's lovely here," Stephie tells her. "That we have an open view."

"I wonder what she'd say about it in November," Aunt Märta says. "When the fog is thickest. She wouldn't think much of the open view then."

Stephie doesn't answer. If Aunt Märta's set her mind on disliking Janice, there's not much she can do about it.

~

Vera and her employer's family are now settled into the shopkeeper's summer rental cottage. As is the custom every year, the island fills up with summer tenants who take over the houses while the fishermen's families move down into their basement rooms. Since the war began, more and more people want to spend the summers in the archipelago. No one can go abroad anymore.

Auntie Alma's summer tenants have three children, two boys and a girl, who's just Nellie's age. Her name is Maud, and she's a tomboy. She goes around in shorts and plays wild games with her brothers. Soon Nellie seems to have forgotten Sonja and her other classmates. She's constantly on the heels of Maud and her brothers, climbing trees, building little houses in the woods, and coming home covered with scrapes and bruises.

Auntie Alma complains to Aunt Märta about Nellie becoming so wild.

"I hardly recognize her. She's always been so nice and neat."

"You've spoiled her, Alma," Aunt Märta says firmly.

"And that always has a price. Speaking of which, you spoil your own children as well."

"How can you say that?" Auntie Alma asks, bewildered. "In any case, Nellie's changed completely. She's suddenly a different girl."

"This, too, shall pass," Aunt Märta comforts her. "She'll settle down again; you'll see."

But Stephie has her doubts. There's something strange about Nellie this summer. Something abrupt and fierce. Stephie hardly recognizes her, either. There's a glare in her eye when she looks at Stephie. Is she still angry about having been slapped, even though Stephie apologized and Nellie accepted her apology? Or is it something else?

Could her own sister hate her?

⁓

Every morning, Stephie goes upstairs to see Miss Björk for her private lessons. They've settled on nine to eleven as their study hours.

They focus on math, physics, and chemistry. It's hard work but fun, especially the math. Every day, Stephie comes back downstairs with homework for the afternoon. In the evenings, she has novels to read for the Swedish literature course. She has a few hours off in the middle of the day to go for a swim.

On Wednesday mornings, Janice gives Stephie an English lesson, which allows Miss Björk to sleep in.

Stephie loves it. She loves reading the poems and short stories by English authors that Janice gives her, and then discussing them in English. Janice teaches Stephie English songs, and sometimes she finds the BBC, an English radio station, when she turns the dial.

Together they listen to news of the war, but it's difficult to get a clear picture of what's going on. The Allied victories in Italy and North Africa seem to have halted. One day, the newscaster informs them in his dry voice that Goebbels, Germany's minister of propaganda, has declared Berlin "free from Jews." When she hears that, Janice turns off the radio.

Janice doesn't give Stephie any homework.

"I'm not a schoolmistress, you know," she says, giving Hedvig Björk a knowing wink.

"Whatever you say," says Miss Björk. "As long as Stephie passes her entrance exam in English. If she doesn't, I'll hold you to blame. And you know what that would mean."

There's a special tone to the conversation between Miss Björk and Janice. Slightly playful but with a serious undertone. *As if everything they say means more than just what the words are telling,* Stephie thinks. *They must be very close friends, in spite of being so different.* Kind of like her and May.

Stephie misses May. She can talk to her about everything. May always listens and understands. She can be serious when necessary, and make a joke at just the right moment. And she would never, ever, betray a confidence.

Vera's different. Although it happened long ago, Stephie remembers how Vera let her down that first year on the island, joining in with the other girls when they bullied Stephie. She'll never trust Vera completely.

It's true that, in Vera's company, Stephie's never bored. Vera laughs and jokes and is full of ideas. But she's kind of different this summer. Sometimes, when she thinks no one's watching, a shadow of fatigue crosses her features. She sometimes goes quiet right in the middle of a conversation, as if she has lost track of the world around her. It's as if there were a second Vera under the bright, happy one. A grown-up Vera Stephie doesn't know.

One day when Vera has the day off and she and Stephie are at the beach, she suddenly gets sick to her stomach. Stephie's just poured their coffee from the thermos. Vera takes her cup, but before she has even a single sip, she puts it down. One hand over her mouth, she rushes into the bushes. Stephie watches her bend over double, vomiting.

"Are you ill?" Stephie asks with concern when Vera returns.

"It's nothing," says Vera. "Probably something I ate. I'm fine now."

20

Midsummer's Eve is the longest day of the year. The sun is high in the sky and stays up longer than any other day.

Since they don't have a globe, Miss Björk uses an old rubber ball to demonstrate to Stephie how the angle of the Earth's axis causes the seasons to change. She runs one of Aunt Märta's knitting needles through the ball and shows Stephie how it rotates around its own axis. At the same time, she orbits it in a wide circle around the lamp that hangs over the table.

"It's like a dance," Miss Björk explains. "Everything is in motion. The whole universe. If it stopped, that would mean death. Movement is life."

But when they step outside after their studies, the

sun isn't even visible. This Midsummer's Eve is a gray day, with rain hanging in the air. Stephie can see there are already showers over the mainland.

"Do you know why it's often not rainy out in the archipelago even when it's raining on the mainland?" Miss Björk asks Stephie.

"No."

"We'll work on that tomorrow, then," her teacher says. "A little meteorology, the study of the weather. Now it's holiday time, so we'll take the rest of the day off."

Janice is sitting outside reading, as she almost always does while Hedvig is teaching Stephie. If the sun is shining, she wears her wide-brimmed straw hat to protect her sensitive skin.

"What a lazy woman!" Aunt Märta mutters. "All she does is read. She could at least do some embroidery."

In Aunt Märta's world, reading isn't for grown-ups. Children read their schoolbooks and the occasional story, while Aunt Märta reads only the newspaper, and a chapter from the Bible every Sunday. That's it.

Janice sets her book in her lap when she hears their voices.

"All done for today?" she asks.

"Yes," Hedvig answers. "Come on. Time for our Midsummer celebrations!"

No one who lives on the island makes much of a fuss about Midsummer. On Easter Eve, there's a bonfire up on the cliffs, but Midsummer has a bad reputation. It's known as a holiday with a lot of drunken rowdiness, and nobody who lives on the island drinks, at least not when anyone else is looking.

But the summer guests always raise a maypole in the meadow above the beach. Stephie goes along with Miss Björk and Janice.

People have already gathered leaves and branches. Maypoles are usually decorated with birch, but there isn't much birch on the island, so ash and bird cherry are also used.

"The main thing is that it's green," says the cheerful woman who has taken charge of the project.

Stephie recognizes her—she's Maud's mother. Theirs is the family renting from Auntie Alma. So Nellie and Maud are probably around, too. Stephie looks for her, but she can't see her.

Maud's mother assigns Stephie and Miss Björk to be flower pickers. They find mostly buttercups, red clover, and a few daisies.

"Where I grew up," says Miss Björk, "we decorated the maypole with daisies, cornflowers, and poppies."

She sounds a bit homesick, and Stephie wonders why she isn't spending her summer up north in Värmland, where her family lives. She certainly hopes Miss Björk hasn't come to the island just for her sake. *No, Janice loves the sea,* Stephie tells herself.

They take their flowers back to the maypole, where they are given one of the wreaths to decorate. Stephie and Miss Björk make little bouquets, and Janice attaches them. They fill the spaces with leaves, since they haven't found enough flowers to cover the entire wreath.

Maud's mother is busy with the other wreath. Suddenly Maud and Nellie appear, at a run. They're disheveled and excited. Maud tears off some leaves from a nearby tree and showers them down over her mother, who just laughs.

"Nellie," Stephie calls. "Come here!"

Nellie comes over to them.

"What is it?"

Her voice sounds sullen, and the gleam in her eye has vanished.

"This is my teacher," says Stephie, "Miss Björk. And her friend Janice. They're our summer tenants, you know." To Miss Björk and Janice, she says, "And this is my younger sister, Nellie."

Nellie shakes hands quite politely.

"Hello, Nellie," says Miss Björk. "When do I get to have you at grammar school? Are you coming in the autumn? Or do you have another year to go?"

"You'll never see me there," Nellie replies. "I'm not going on after sixth grade."

"What about your friend, then?" asks Miss Björk. "Is she not going to grammar school, either?"

"Maud?" Nellie asks. "That's a different story. She lives in town. She's starting this fall, though she doesn't really want to. She's thinking about running away to work on a farm as a stable hand. She's wild about horses."

When Nellie talks about Maud, her whole face lights up. Her eyes gleam, and a lock of hair falls across her forehead. When she shakes her head, she actually looks like an impatient little pony with a black mane.

"I've got to go now," she says. "Maud's waiting. We just came to tell her mamma Auntie Alma made us sandwiches, so she needn't come home to give us lunch."

She curtsies quickly in the direction of Miss Björk and Janice, and runs off.

"What a great little sister," Janice says to Stephie. "So lively and energetic!"

"I wouldn't worry," says Miss Björk. "She's sure to change her mind about school. She just needs some time to mature."

If only that were true, Stephie thinks. *And if only my sole worry about her had to do with her education.*

But she doesn't talk to Miss Björk and Janice about it. She can't share her worries about Nellie with anyone. It's no one's business but her own, and Mamma's and Papa's.

Oh, how she wishes she could talk to Mamma and Papa! Just for a couple of hours, to unburden herself and tell them how heavily her sense of responsibility for Nellie weighs on her. If only she dared to write to them about how things really are, and if only they could write a real letter back, not just thirty words.

There are so many things she wishes she could talk with them about, especially with Mamma. She remembers their long afternoon chats when she used to come home from school. They talked about her day, her teachers, her classmates, about birthday parties and outings. Now that Stephie's older, they would talk about different things, of course. About love, and growing up, and the important things in life.

She has Aunt Märta, Auntie Tyra, and Miss Björk. But none of them knows her the way Mamma does. None of them read bedtime stories to Stephie and sat with her when she couldn't fall asleep. None of them nursed her through the measles or held her hand on the first day of school. They mean a great deal to her, each in her own way, and she knows they care for her.

But they can never replace her mamma.

21

That afternoon, they dance around the maypole to accordion music and sing. In the circle, Stephie grasps Miss Björk's hand in her right one, and with her left, she holds onto the little daughter of one of the summer guests. She joins in the singing as best she can.

> *I saw her yesterday evening*
> *Out in the bright moonlight.*
> *Everyone picks a girl.*
> *I pick one, too,*
> *And if you're last, you're out.*

Bewildered, she watches as everyone quickly picks a partner. Miss Björk and Janice laugh and hug. The little girl finds her mother and runs into her arms. Stephie's the last one out, all alone.

Poor her, poor on her
Nobody picked her.

Suddenly, Miss Björk takes Stephie by the hand and pulls her in. They make a little circle of three—Stephie, Miss Björk, and Janice.

"It's a silly game," Hedvig Björk whispers. "Nobody should ever be left out."

~

After the maypole dancing, they go home. That evening there's going to be a dance in the harbor on one of the nearby islands. Stephie wonders if Vera is planning to go. She didn't come down to the maypole even though it's Wednesday and she ought to have the day off.

"Tonight you're supposed to pick seven kinds of flowers, you know," says Miss Björk.

"Seven kinds of flowers?"

"Yes, and put them under your pillow. Then you'll dream about the man you're going to marry. But, of course, a good student like you ought to identify the flowers by genus and species first."

Stephie laughs. "I'll be sure to do that."

At the turn in the road that leads to the shop, they run into Vera. Miss Björk and Janice continue on home.

Stephie and Vera sit down on the stone wall, side by side.

"Are you going to the dance tonight?" Stephie asks.

Vera shakes her head.

"Don't you have the day off?"

"I do," says Vera. "But just look at me."

Stephie looks at Vera, who appears the way she always does, except maybe that her face is a little chubbier and her blouse seems to be pulling across her chest.

"You look fine," says Stephie. "But if you're not going dancing, maybe you'd like to come and pick flowers with me tonight?"

"Pick flowers?"

Stephie explains the custom. Vera didn't know about putting flowers under your pillow, either. But after listening to Stephie, she shakes her head again.

"No, there's no point in my doing it."

"Don't you want to know who you're going to marry?"

"Good grief, Stephie," says Vera. Then she promises to go along and pick flowers after all.

⚬

You're supposed to pick the flowers in silence when the Midsummer Night, never truly black, is at its darkest. So later that evening, Stephie and Vera stumble around in the dusky night, hunting out their seven different kinds. It's not easy to find so many on this island, with its stony terrain. In the end, they each have six: buttercups, bitter vetch, clover, tufted vetch, crimson cranesbill, and babies' slippers. They don't pick the German catchfly growing on the verge since the sticky stalks would stain their pillows.

Vera points to a flower bed outside one of the houses, where there are plenty of bleeding hearts and peonies growing.

Stephie shakes her head. The flowers have to be wild.

In a crevice, they spy something blue and purple. Wild pansies—the island's signature flower.

Carefully, they each pick one of the little pansies. Now tradition demands that they go home without either talking or laughing.

Vera starts to tease Stephie, making funny faces and joking around. When that doesn't make Stephie laugh, Vera starts doing some of her old showpieces. She mimes the shopkeeper's affectations, the way he fusses over the customers, and she acts out the postmistress and her nosiness, doing all this without saying a word.

Stephie presses her lips together as hard as she can. She is not going to laugh!

By the time they come to the crossroads where they go their separate ways, Stephie's face is bright red with the effort. They part without a word.

As Stephie tiptoes to the kitchen settle in the basement, where she's sleeping all summer, she's as quiet as a mouse so she won't wake Aunt Märta. The sky is already brightening toward the east, by the mainland. The shortest night of the year is over.

Although Stephie is tired, she can't fall asleep. She wonders whether Miss Björk and Janice have flowers under their pillows, too. Neither of them is married. But Stephie doesn't think Miss Björk really wants to get married. She has a job, a nice apartment, and her girls at school.

What about Janice? She looks so romantic. Stephie's sure she receives huge bouquets of roses from secret admirers at the ballet, and goes out to supper with elegant gentlemen late in the evenings after her performances.

Ballerinas probably can't marry and have children. Not unless they give up dancing, Stephie thinks. *The same way an opera singer has to choose between her career and having a family.*

Stephie sighs. "If Mamma never gets to sing the Queen of the Night, I'm to blame," she says softly.

The idea strikes Stephie like a bolt of lightning. She's never thought of Mamma that way before. Mamma's always been Mamma, not a person with dreams and desires of her own. Of course Stephie is aware that Mamma had a life before she met Papa, married him, and had children. That she learned to play the piano and took singing lessons from a very early age. That she sang her first big role at the opera at just nineteen, and that everyone predicted she would have a brilliant career. And that she quit the opera after four years because she was pregnant.

örk says they are more truthful, too. Because
the Swedes call their neutrality, the Swedish
ies still censor the news bulletins.

; neutral implies not taking a stand. Sweden
o stay out of the war at any price.

reight cars carry iron ore to the German ar-
s industry from northern Swedish mines. And
ains pass, too, full of German soldiers on their
and from occupied Norway. Many people are
set about those trains full of Germans, and
mand that they not be permitted to cross Swe-

you know what the local stationmaster here said
Germans?" May asks Stephie.

has two weeks of vacation from the laundry
he is working this summer. She and Stephie
ad to foot on the kitchen settle. Every midday,
to the beach and lie in the sun on the cliffs.
ather is lovely, with the sun shining over the

what?"

ain from Germany stopped and some Germans
eir heads out the windows. 'Is this Gote-Burg?'
outed. 'Gote-Burg?' the stationmaster answered.
ate to tell you, but it's Stalingrad,' he said."
ie laughs.

can imagine how fast they pulled those heads of
ack in," May says, giggling.

Does getting married and having children necessarily
mean having to give up what you want most of all?

Mamma had planned to take up her singing again
when Stephie and Nellie were bigger. She went on taking lessons, and singing at home and among friends.
But the year Nellie started school, the Nazis came to
power in Vienna. The opera was closed to Jewish sing-
ers and musicians. Mamma wasn't even allowed to sit in
the audience and watch her former colleagues perform.

*Now she's in Theresienstadt. And she didn't get to sing
there, either. Why?*

Eventually, Stephie falls asleep. She is still sleeping
deeply when Aunt Märta brings her a cup of coffee
in bed. She doesn't remember anything she may have
dreamed.

22

The card from Papa takes a very long time to arrive. It's dated May 17, but Stephie doesn't receive it until the end of June.

Theresienstadt, 17 May 1943

Dear Stephie!
 It is a great comfort that you want to continue your schooling and can. It is the only way to get anywhere in life. Mamma sang yesterday. Wonderful!
                    Papa

Mamma sang yesterday. This must mean that the performance of *The Magic Flute* took place. Whatever was

crossed out in Papa's last card
it after all!

Stephie wishes Papa had writ
singing, instead of urging Step
He doesn't seem to realize th
That she knows what's best fo

She was just a child when the
who looked up to her parent
them. Now she's almost sixtee
what it would be like to be w
way. Get to know them differe

But she cannot. Not until th

Perhaps it won't be long now.
lies at Stalingrad and in North
further victories. In July, they
the Eastern Front, the German
but the Russians stop their prog
westward.

Stephie, Miss Björk, and Jan
one day to the next. Aunt Mär
listen to the evening news at s
ice is able to get the English BB
dials on the old radio. The room
swishing sound, and fragments o
guages. Now and then, German
Janice silences them with a quick

The BBC has more detailed re

"Where did you hear that one?"

"Papa heard it down at the shipyard. Somebody read it in the paper. He says it's a true story."

May's papa always has stories to tell about his co-workers or the foremen at the shipyard, or about something he saw on the tram. The stories are often critical of the people he calls "the powers that be." Laughing at people with authority makes life easier to bear for people who are powerless themselves.

Vera's the same, Stephie thinks. *She imitates and jokes about people so she won't have to be scared of them.*

"Let's swim," says May.

"I wonder if Vera's going to turn up," Stephie says. "She has the afternoon off today."

"I don't think she'll want to be seen in a bathing suit much longer," says May.

"Why not?"

"Didn't you notice last night?" May asks. "Didn't you see her tightening her belt so it wouldn't show?"

"What are you talking about? So what wouldn't show?"

May just stares at her.

"Stephanie," she says. "I know you aren't always very aware of these things, but are you trying to tell me you really don't know?"

"What don't I know?"

Stephie raises her voice. It annoys her that May is acting all superior, pretending to know more about Vera than she does. Vera is Stephie's friend, not May's, although they do get along better now than they used to.

"That she's in the family way," May says calmly. "Surely you've noticed?"

Stephie can't believe her ears. "Of course she's not," she replies. "Where did you get that from?"

May doesn't say anything, but Stephie can tell from the look in her eyes that May is certain. She wasn't just making it up.

Vera was sick to her stomach recently. She's getting chubbier. She mentioned herself that she looked different. And the creaking bed in the cabin that night . . .

Stephie feels foolish. Silly and childish. How could she not have understood? And she considers herself Vera's best friend!

"Are you sure?"

"Just ask her," says May. "I can't believe she hasn't talked to you about it. Her best friend. I would have told you right away. But of course I'd never have gotten myself into that predicament."

She sounds so dreadfully sensible, as if she thinks she is a better person than Vera.

"It's his fault just as much as hers," says Stephie.

"Oh, yes," says May. "Don't be angry. Come on, let's take a swim."

23

It's Sunday morning, and Aunt Märta is getting ready to go to church, when May has an idea. Aunt Märta is wearing her navy-blue Sunday dress, and her bun is pulled tight at the back of her head. She's standing at the mirror, fastening her straw hat with hat pins.

Stephie usually goes with her to church. She does it to make Aunt Märta happy. When they arrive at the prayer house arm in arm, Aunt Märta always looks so proud. But Stephie is ashamed. She doesn't really believe in the things they preach. She doesn't even think the songs are very nice anymore.

This Sunday, Aunt Märta has to go alone. It's May's last day on the island. After dinner, Stephie's going to walk her to the steamboat.

"Do they take up collection at your church?" May asks Aunt Märta.

Aunt Märta turns to look at May.

"Certainly. It usually goes to our missions in heathen countries."

"I was wondering," May said, "and I hope you won't be offended. I know you and Stephie send packages to her parents, and that they need both food and clothing. I was wondering whether one week's collection could be used for them? Everyone here knows Stephie and Nellie."

Aunt Märta nods thoughtfully. "That's not a bad idea. What do you say, Stephie?"

Charity. Isn't it shameful enough that she has to live on money that comes from the goodwill of people who contribute to the relief committee? Is she going to have to beg for money for Mamma and Papa now, too?

But she swallows her pride. It *is* a good idea. It will soon be autumn and then winter again. Perhaps they could buy warm overcoats for her parents. And shoes, too, if they can collect enough ration coupons.

"Yes," Stephie says. "That would be good."

"I'll have a word with the pastor," says Aunt Märta, "and we'll see what he says."

❧

After Aunt Märta leaves, Stephie and May go out into the garden. Miss Björk and Janice are sitting at the table in their bathrobes, having their morning tea.

"Hi, girls," says Miss Björk. "Would you like some tea?"

May hesitates. She hasn't quite gotten used to spending time with her teacher outside of school.

"Yes, please," says Stephie.

She gets two cups. Janice pours and puts in the sugar for them. That's how it's done in England, as she has told Stephie. One of their English lessons was a little tea party at which Stephie pretended to be the lady of the house, offering her guests, Janice and Miss Björk, tea, sugar and milk, buns and scones.

May sips at her tea, wrinkling her nose.

"Don't you care for tea, May?" Janice asks.

"I'm not sure," says May. "I expected it to taste more like coffee."

"We had a morning dip," says Miss Björk. "From the jetty. A nice hot cup of tea tastes wonderful after a swim. Now we're going for a long walk on the beach. Would you like to join us? We could collect maritime plants for your herbariums."

Janice laughs. "Come now, Hedvig," she says. "Let the girls have some time off. You're going home today, May, aren't you?"

"That's right," says Stephie. "I think we'll stay here. We promised to have coffee ready for Aunt Märta when she comes back from church."

Half an hour later, Miss Björk and Janice head off, dressed in shorts and sneakers. Miss Björk is carrying a collecting box and a small net. Janice has a book in her shoulder bag.

Stephie and May sit in the sun on the steps, watching them walk off.

"I saw them this morning," May says, once they are out of earshot. "They were swimming in the nude."

"I know," says Stephie. "They skinny-dip in the mornings. Aunt Märta doesn't approve, but she doesn't want to reprimand them. At least when Uncle Evert's at home, they wear their suits."

"They seem to be such good friends," says May. "Just like girlfriends, except grown up. I hope we'll be like that! We could share an apartment. You'd study medicine and I'd study social work. When we're done, maybe we could both work in child health care."

She takes off her glasses and rubs her nose, as she always does when she gets excited about something.

"I might not stay here," says Stephie. "Once the war is over."

"Even if your parents could join you?"

"I don't know," says Stephie. "I'm not sure if I belong here or in Vienna. Or anywhere."

May sits quietly. "If you leave," she says finally, "I will never have another friend like you."

She puts her glasses back on. Behind them, her eyes are brimming.

"Me too," says Stephie. "No other friend could be like you. Still, I might have to go."

May reaches out. Carefully, her fingertips brush Stephie's cheek. Stephie puts her own hand on top of May's, holding it on her cheek.

"It's funny," says May. "Until I met you, I always felt lonely. Of course I have my folks, and all my brothers and sisters, and the kids in the building, and my classmates at elementary school. But I always felt different. Then we met, and though you're completely different than I am, it's like we've known each other all our lives. It's odd, isn't it?"

Stephie nods. "Soul mates," she says, "that's what we are."

May looks at her. "Could I put my head on your lap?"

Stephie nods. May moves down a couple of steps and leans back toward Stephie. Her head feels heavy. Gently, Stephie strokes her hair. They sit there for a long time and forget to get the coffee ready. When they hear Aunt Märta's bicycle tires coming down the gravelly hill, they jump up and rush into the kitchen.

 ❧

After dinner, Stephie rides May on her bike down to the harbor. May sits on the clamp, and her suitcase hangs from the handlebars. It's heavy-going on the hills, and on the steepest one they have to get off. May pushes the bike.

Close to the shop, they meet Sylvia, the shopkeeper's daughter who was so cruel to Stephie her first year on the island. She hardly acknowledges them, just raises her eyebrows and nods almost imperceptibly.

"Didn't she go to our school?" May asks when Sylvia has passed.

"Yes," says Stephie. "She started when we did. But grammar school was too much for her. She switched to secretarial school instead."

Stephie feels a rush of triumph when she says that. She's never forgiven Sylvia.

"What does she have to look so stuck-up about, then?" asks May.

"Her father's the shopkeeper," Stephie tells her. "Most of the men on the island are fishermen. The few who don't walk around in dirty blue overalls think they're better. And Sylvia certainly thinks she's better than people like us."

People like us.

After four years in Sweden, Stephie has nearly forgotten that she once lived in a big, beautiful apartment with soft carpets and antique furniture. That she and Nellie had a large, bright nursery, and Papa had a study full of books. If they had still been living there, she would never have known anyone like May. Or anyone like Vera.

They coast down the last slope to the harbor area. There are already people waiting by the steamboat landing. Stephie and May carry the suitcase together, each holding one of the handles, as they walk out onto the dock.

Now the steamboat whistles as it sets course for the jetty. Stephie and May hug.

"See you in three weeks," says Stephie.

Three weeks from today, May's whole family is coming to spend Sunday on the island. The little ones will get to swim, and May's parents and Aunt Märta are finally going to meet.

Stephie stays on the dock, waving until May becomes a small dot next to the railing.

24

"Why haven't you said anything?"

Stephie's upset. Until the very last, she went on hoping that May was wrong. But Vera doesn't deny it. It's true, she is expecting. In January.

"I don't know," Vera replies. "I guess I figured you'd find out in due time."

"But what will you do?"

"Rikard and I are engaged," Vera tells her. "Look, here's my ring."

Stephie hasn't noticed the thin gold band on Vera's left ring finger until now.

"So we'll be getting married, come fall."

"Getting married? You're only sixteen."

"We'll need a special permit, of course," Vera continues. "But I understand that's not a problem if you're pregnant."

"But what about all the things you were planning to do? Be a movie star? Get famous?"

"A child's dreams," says Vera. "Anyway, it's too late now."

She looks tired. Her face is a little puffy and her pretty red hair is dull and uncombed.

Stephie is outraged. Although she never believed in Vera's movie-star dreams, she feels as if Vera is giving up now. As if she feels her life is over. Unless . . .

She has to ask.

"Do you love him?"

"Love," says Vera. "That's the kind of thing you hear in the movies, too. He's kind. He wants to take care of me and the kid. And once he gets his engineering degree, he'll be making good money."

"How can you?" Stephie cries. "Are you going to marry him because he's kind?"

Vera looks her in the eye. There's a bit of her old obstinacy in her gaze.

"Any other suggestions? You always know best, don't you?"

Stephie bites her lip.

"I'm not going to get some phony doctor to get rid of it," Vera goes on, "and maybe ruin me for life in the bargain. And I don't want my kid growing up without a papa, like I did. Do you think it's been easy being the only illegitimate child on this island? Someone people always look down on?"

"What if you had the baby," Stephie says slowly, "and then . . ."

"Gave it up?" Vera fills in. "I never expected to have to hear that from you, of all people! You ought to know better. You've been given up, haven't you?"

Stephie is quiet. Everything Vera is saying is true. And yet it all feels wrong. There's no way out.

"Oh, Vera," she says. "I'm so sorry."

"No need to be," Vera says curtly. "He's a good person. We'll be fine. I'm glad he wants to take care of us."

"Of course he does!" Stephie exclaims. "It's his child, too, not just yours."

"Right," says Vera. "That's how it is."

❧

Uncle Evert is pale and solemn. He's at the table in the basement kitchen, spreading margarine on a piece of crispbread. Stephie sees that the hand holding the knife is trembling.

It's happened again. A fishing boat from the island has been blown up by a mine. This time, though, the whole crew survived. They were taken on board by other nearby fishing vessels.

"A hairsbreadth from death," says Uncle Evert. "No one can live like this for very long. They were in Swedish territorial waters, too. Just like the *Wolf*."

Stephie has goose bumps. The *Wolf* lies on the seabed not far from the island, her crew still down there, too, for the moment. She's going to be towed ashore. Divers are currently working out how to proceed. They'll bring her to port before the summer ends.

"Sometimes I wonder," Uncle Evert goes on, "whether I ought to sell the *Diana*. Take a job on shore."

"Sell the *Diana*?" Aunt Märta's voice nearly cracks. "You can't be serious!"

"Well," says Uncle Evert, "I have always known that the sea giveth and the sea taketh away. I can live with that. But those awful metal mines lying there, just under the water, waiting to get us, well . . . knowing that people put them there to kill us is what I can't bear. What if I were to die? What would become of you? And our girl?"

"We'll have no talk of such things here," says Aunt Märta. "Particularly not with our girl in the room."

Our girl, our girl. Speaking of her as if she were a child. Talking over her head.

"Please don't sell the *Diana*!" Stephie pleads. "Please, please, Uncle Evert. The war's almost over. It just has to end soon."

Uncle Evert's sea blue eyes look at her mournfully.

"We must hope so, dear child," he says. "We must hope so."

"This is Judith."

The voice at the other end of the line sounds distant but excited.

"It's Judith Liebermann. You haven't forgotten me?"

"Of course not. But how did you find this phone number?"

"The operator helped me," says Judith. "You mentioned that your foster parents were named Jansson. Who was that who answered, anyway? She sounded so young."

"That was my homeroom teacher," Stephie explains. "She and a friend of hers are our summer tenants this year."

Stephie is standing in the hall, by the stairs up to the bedrooms. Miss Björk goes out and closes the door to the sitting room so Stephie can talk in private. It's a hot day. The receiver in her hand grows sticky with sweat.

"How are things? Are you working this summer?" Stephie asks.

The chocolate factory must be even worse than usual in this heat. Stephie tries to imagine Judith, pale and nauseated in the stuffy, sooty, chocolate-scented air.

"I'm on vacation now," Judith tells her, "this week and next. Yesterday Susie and I took the tram to the end of the line and swam out at Saltholmen. But they charge so much for the bathhouse. And now Susie is being sent to some family in the country for three weeks. Almost all the Children's Home girls are away somewhere. There are only four of us left."

"Why don't you come here?" Stephie asks. "At least for a couple of days."

"Do you think that would be all right? With your foster parents, I mean."

"I'm sure it will. I'll ask Aunt Märta."

Stephie promises to call Judith back after she's talked to Aunt Märta.

She has mixed feelings. Of course it would be nice to have company, now that May's back at her laundry job and Vera is becoming quieter and more withdrawn as her stomach bulges. Soon she'll have to wear corsets and special gathered skirts to conceal her bump. And just as May predicted, Vera doesn't put on her bathing suit anymore.

On the other hand, Stephie needs time on her own, to study. May was very understanding about her schoolwork, but it would be different with Judith.

And there's something else bothering her. She's afraid that Aunt Märta and Judith won't get along.

Stephie decides she mustn't worry. She remembers having the same thoughts the first time May was coming to the island. But May and Aunt Märta got along just fine, in spite of their very different opinions. It might be the same with Judith.

"What kind of a girl is she?" Aunt Märta asks.

"She's from Vienna," Stephie tells her. "We were in the same class there."

"Why is she at the Children's Home? Wasn't there a family to take her in?"

"She lived with a family in the country to begin with. Then she moved into town for a job. At the chocolate factory."

That's not really the full story of Judith's time in Sweden. But if Aunt Märta knew how many times Judith had to change foster families, she would think there was something wrong with her.

"All right," says Aunt Märta. "For a couple of days, then. Monday to Wednesday? Will that suit?"

25

Aunt Märta spoke to the pastor about taking up a collection for Stephie and Nellie's parents. He wasn't prepared to say yes or no on his own, but he promised to invite the girls along to a meeting of the church elders to present the idea.

Nellie refuses to go.

"No," she says, pinching her lips together. "Stephie can do it."

Aunt Märta and Auntie Alma try to persuade her. Stephie knows what they're thinking. A cute eleven-year-old with long braids, who sings like an angel in the church children's choir to boot, would give a more sympathetic impression than a skinny sixteen-year-old who almost got herself thrown out of the congregation for her "sinful way of life" in town.

But Nellie stubbornly refuses. No attempts to convince her, no threats or bribes, make her change her mind. Stephie is furious with her, but still, she admires her for the strength of her convictions.

"No. No. No."

In the end, Stephie and Aunt Märta go to the meeting by themselves.

It's held in the very same room where Stephie once had to defend herself for having gone to the movies. The same people are there, too. Five men, one woman. And the pastor with his big hands.

At least this time, Stephie is invited to sit down. The pastor asks her to explain why she has come.

"My parents are in a camp," Stephie begins. "Theresienstadt, near Prague. They had to leave behind everything we owned in Vienna. They need food and warm clothing. I think my papa's managing all right, but Mamma's quite sickly. She had pneumonia back in Vienna and nearly died. If this is a cold winter, I'm afraid she'll get sick again."

Her voice falters. She isn't used to talking about her parents in front of strangers.

"Stephie and I send food boxes," Aunt Märta adds. "We send what we can afford, and stretch our ration cards as far as they will go. But if we had a couple of hundred crowns extra for clothes and shoes, that would be very helpful."

"Remind me," the woman says. "Your parents aren't Christian, are they?"

"No," says Stephie. "They're Jewish."

"Would it be possible for them to be baptized at the camp?"

Stephie can't believe her ears. Here she is talking about cold winters, hunger, and illness, and the lady suggests that her parents change their religion!

"If they were Christian," the woman goes on, "I'm sure it would be easier for us to help them. We have an Israel mission that could take on their case."

"And another thing," one of the men says. "Aren't there thousands of prisoners in those camps? And aren't there camps all over Europe? With different kinds of prisoners in them, besides the Jews. Prisoners of conscience. Christians, even. And there are civilians, too, suffering because of the war. We can't help everyone."

"That's true" says the pastor. "We can't help everyone."

"No," says the woman. "And there are suffering people closer to home as well."

Their voices echo in a vacuum around Stephie. Unreal, alien. She feels as if she is about to burst into tears. Her throat thickens. But she's not going to let them see her cry.

"But we can still help a few," Aunt Märta says. "We can help this child's parents. Isn't that good enough?"

"Let us think about it," says the pastor. "We'll consider the matter and seek counsel. We can discuss it again in a week or two. All right?"

No! Stephie wants to shout. *That's not all right at*

all! But she knows that if she tries to say a single word, she'll cry.

↜

The weekend before Judith is due to visit, British planes bomb Hamburg, one of the largest cities in Germany. The radio newscasters call the bombing a firestorm over Hamburg, and report thousands of people dead.

Stephie has celebrated the Allied victories in the war all spring and summer, but this bombing brings her no joy. *Is it really necessary to kill thousands of civilians to bring this war to an end?*

"Yes, it is," Judith tells her. "The British know what they're doing. And the Germans bombed English cities early in the war, didn't they? Not to mention that the German people voted for Hitler and started this war."

"Not all the German people," says Stephie.

"Are you feeling sorry for them? After all the harm they've done to you and your family?"

They're making their way across the island. Stephie has just picked up Judith in the harbor and has her little suitcase hanging over the handlebars of her bike as she leads it. Judith is walking on the other side of the bicycle. She's just as pale as ever, but her freckles stand out more against her skin than they did last spring.

"Have you heard from your parents again, since you had that letter returned?"

"Yes," says Stephie. "One card from Papa. But it was quite a while ago now."

"Do you write to them?"

Stephie nods. "Every week. Just like I always have since we got here."

"And no more of your letters have been returned?"

"No."

"Good," says Judith. "As long as they're still at Theresienstadt, there is nothing to worry about. Are we almost there?"

"Not quite. Would you like me to ride you on the back of the bike?"

Judith gives Stephie's red bicycle a suspicious look.

"Can you?"

"Sure," Stephie replies.

"No, I'd rather walk," says Judith. "Whose bike is that, anyway?"

"Mine."

"Yours? Your own?"

"It was my thirteenth birthday present from Aunt Märta and Uncle Evert."

Judith looks thoughtful.

"They must be very special people," she says, "to give their foster child such a nice present."

"Yes," Stephie agrees, "they are very special people."

She'd like to add, *They've given me other things that are more important than this bike.* But she doesn't want to sound high-flown.

Judith introduces herself politely to Aunt Märta and shakes her hand. But she has a suspicious look in her eye. Judith doesn't trust Swedish people. Perhaps she doesn't trust anyone.

And Aunt Märta inspects Judith, too, giving her long frizzy hair and her freckles a skeptical look.

"So I understand you're a factory worker, Judith," she says.

"At a chocolate factory," says Judith. "Kanold's, in Gårda."

Dinner is already on the table, in two serving dishes with upside-down plates on top of them to keep the food warm. Stephie peeks under one of the plates and sees, to her relief, that it's boiled cod. She forgot to tell Aunt Märta that Judith won't eat pork, because it's against her religion. She'll tell her later, when Judith isn't listening, so Aunt Märta doesn't serve pork and beans or blood pudding tomorrow.

But when they are at the table and have uncovered the serving dishes, Aunt Märta walks over to the stove and picks up a skillet.

"Wait!" Stephie cries.

"What for?" Aunt Märta is holding the skillet over the bowl, about to pour the contents over the cod. Contents that smell unmistakably of bacon.

Boiled cod is everyday fare on the island. When Aunt

Märta wants to make it a little festive, she crumbles some bacon to put over the top, along with the fat.

"Judith doesn't eat pork." Stephie blushes.

She's embarrassed in both directions. For not having told Aunt Märta in advance, and because Judith will realize that Stephie has been eating pork for four years without objecting.

"That's all right," says Judith. "If you don't mind, Mrs. Jansson, I'll just serve myself before you pour the sauce over the fish."

She glances at Stephie, who looks away.

"Help yourself," says Aunt Märta, passing the dish of cod to Judith.

Her tone of voice really says, *What a way to behave! You should eat what's put before you.*

They eat their dinner in silence. The bacon, which Stephie usually enjoys, sticks in her throat.

26

The first evening has gone all right. Stephie and Judith sit on the jetty, watching the sun set over the sea and talking.

"Isn't it beautiful?" Stephie asks, with a gesture toward the colorful drama in the west.

"I suppose," says Judith, "but it's so empty. I prefer to see buildings, and other people."

"When I first got here," Stephie tells her, "I thought it was awful. The end of the world. Nothing but sea and stone. But now I like it. Isn't that strange?"

"Yes," Judith agrees. "I don't think I could ever get used to living like this. Though I know there are no big cities in Palestine, either. My brothers live on a kibbutz."

"A what?"

"A farm everyone owns collectively," Judith explains. "After the war, I'm going there. I guess it will take some getting used to for me, too. But all I want is to be with my own people."

She goes silent, staring out over the sea.

"It is quite beautiful, really," she says finally.

The next morning, Stephie goes upstairs to have her lessons with Miss Björk as usual. Judith promises to do the breakfast dishes and make the beds, chores Stephie normally does before going upstairs.

When she comes back out, Judith is in the garden, sitting with Janice, who is teaching her to count to ten in English.

"Wan, too, sri," Judith says with difficulty.

Janice laughs. "After the war," she says, "everyone's going to have to learn English. It's going to be the new world language. German will become a dead language, like Latin."

"Don't exaggerate," says Miss Björk. "Hitler's Germany is going to lose the war, but the Germans aren't going to die out. And remember, German is these girls' mother tongue. Come along, Janice, I'm longing for a swim."

Hedvig Björk and Janice have found a little out-of-the-way cove where no one else goes. They skinny-dip from the cliffs there, all day.

"Will you join us, girls?" asks Miss Björk.

"I don't think so," Stephie is quick to reply.

She can't imagine how Judith would react to the skinny-dipping.

"I think we'll go to the regular beach," Stephie says. "I want to show Judith around the island, too."

On her way to the beach, Stephie makes her usual stop at the post office. She hasn't heard from Mamma or Papa for six weeks now. There's no card today, either.

"I'm sure you'll get one soon," Judith comforts her. "You know how slow the mail service can be."

As they leave the post office, they bump into Vera, who is on her way in.

"Vera, I'd like you to meet Judith Liebermann from Vienna," Stephie says.

Vera inspects Judith's curly hair and translucent skin, while Judith can't help staring at Vera's protruding belly.

"Do you have tomorrow night off?" Stephie asks.

Vera nods.

"I'll come by for you," says Stephie, "after I see Judith off at the boat."

She wants to make it clear to Vera that Judith isn't staying long. She remembers how jealous Vera was the first time May visited her.

"Fine," says Vera. "Time for me to collect the mail. The lady of the house won't get out of bed until she's read the newspaper and the day's letters."

"She's getting married in the fall," Stephie hurries to say as soon as Vera is out of earshot. She doesn't want Judith to get the impression that Vera's some little tramp who got pregnant by mistake. But Judith doesn't seem very interested.

"I see" is all she says.

Out on the cliffs, Stephie sees Sylvia, the shop-keeper's daughter, and her friend Barbro, so she stays on the beach even though she prefers swimming from the cliffs.

They spread out their towels on the gravelly sand and lie in the sun, which is very strong that day.

"Come on," Stephie says after a few minutes. "Let's swim!"

Side by side, they run down to the shore and out into the water. But when they get in up to their knees, Judith slows down and treads carefully, one step at a time.

"Does it get very deep?" she asks.

"Not for a while," Stephie tells her. "The shallow part's pretty big."

Soon she's in up to her chest and waiting impatiently for Judith.

"Come on!"

Judith takes a couple of hesitant steps toward her. Stephie takes her hands and pulls her on. Then she throws herself into the water and swims a few strokes, expecting Judith to swim alongside her. But Judith doesn't come along. Stephie turns back in her direction.

Behind her, Judith's head emerges from the water, her hair dripping around her face and shoulders. She's spitting and hissing, blowing water out of her nose and mouth. Her blue eyes are terrified.

"What do you think you're doing?" Judith shouts. "Trying to drown me?"

"Sorry," says Stephie. "Did you lose your footing?"

Then it strikes her. Judith doesn't know how to swim.

When they stay in the shallow area, like little children, Judith is happy again, splashing and playing. Stephie sees Sylvia and Barbro watching them and giggling.

But she doesn't care. It no longer matters what Sylvia thinks of her.

❧

That evening, Stephie and Judith go upstairs to listen to the news on the radio. But there isn't much about the war, and after a short time, Miss Björk turns the radio off.

"Do you want to show your friend around?" she asks. "This is your home, after all."

Stephie thanks Miss Björk and takes Judith another flight up.

"This is my bedroom," she tells her, opening the door to the room directly under the roof. "I mean, when we don't have summer tenants."

Judith walks into the narrow room, with Stephie behind her.

It smells stuffy, but everything looks as usual. The bed, the chair, the dresser.

And the painting of Jesus.

Stephie sees it at the same moment Judith does. Over the dresser, hanging from its nail.

Jesus, arms outstretched, in a light red mantle, with rays of light around him and a halo over his head.

Judith stares at the painting, and then at Stephie.

"What have they done to you?" she asks. "Did they force you to convert to Christianity?"

Force her? Well, maybe. But she went along with it. She never refused. She didn't dare to object. She let herself be baptized, she went to Sunday school, and she sang their songs and prayed their prayers. She did.

"They didn't have to force me," says Stephie. "I was willing to do what they wanted me to do."

"How could you?" asks Judith. "How could you betray your own people?"

27

The rest of the evening and the next morning, Judith is withdrawn and quiet. At breakfast, she says she's decided to take the ten o'clock boat back to Göteborg.

"You don't need to walk me, I know the way now."

Judith's disappointment stands between them like a wall. Stephie can't find a crack. They say good-bye to each other as formally as if they were strangers. Stephie stands at the gate watching Judith walk away resolutely, suitcase in hand.

"What's gotten into her?" Aunt Märta asks. "Did you have an argument?"

"No," says Stephie, "not exactly."

How could she possibly explain to Aunt Märta?

She ponders it all day herself. Was Judith right? Has

she betrayed her own people? Has she betrayed Mamma and Papa?

She remembers the pastor and the council of elders. Their unsympathetic looks when she explained her parents' need of help. The pastor's way of clasping his hands in prayer.

What does she have in common with them?

What does she have in common with their sugary sweet Jesus?

Slowly, a decision begins to take root.

≈

As evening approaches, Stephie remembers she promised to call for Vera. It's Wednesday, Vera's evening off.

At six-thirty she knocks on the kitchen door of the shopkeeper's summer cottage. It doesn't open for a long time, and the person who opens it isn't Vera. It's the lady of the house herself.

"No, Vera's not in," she says. "I believe she went for a walk. But you're welcome to come in and wait in her room."

Stephie walks behind Vera's employer through the kitchen and to Vera's bedroom. It's really more like a walk-in closet with a bed in it, along with a tiny dresser and a rib-backed wooden chair with one broken leg.

The door shuts behind her and Stephie sits down. Vera's sure to be back soon. They always spend Wednesday evenings together.

But it gets later. The clock on the kitchen wall ticks noisily, and after a while, she hears it strike seven. Stephie is getting impatient. She leafs through an old magazine she finds on the dresser. A magazine clipping falls to the floor. Stephie leans down to pick it up.

There's a picture of a girl leaning back, her hair cascading over her bare shoulders. Her blouse is mostly unbuttoned, revealing her round breasts almost entirely. Her hands are pulling at the blouse as if she wants to take it off. Her mouth is open, her eyes half shut.

At first Stephie doesn't want to believe it. But she recognizes the reclining girl in the picture beyond a doubt.

The girl in the photograph is Vera.

That photographer. The one who was going to make Vera a famous movie star. So this is the kind of picture he was taking!

It would have been nice if you'd come along. The example from German class shoots through Stephie's mind like a bolt of lightning.

If she had just gone along with Vera to the photographer's studio, this would never have happened. She would have pulled Vera out of there faster than anything.

Stephie feels like tearing up the picture and forgetting that it ever existed. But it's been cut from a magazine. That means it must have been printed in thousands of copies. Thousands and thousands of people must have seen it. Thousands of men gaping at Vera's body, just as

Bengt's hands had crawled over her own body on the cabin porch.

Stephie's so upset she doesn't hear the footsteps approaching through the kitchen. She doesn't even react until the door opens, and then it's too late. Vera has already seen what she's holding in her hand.

"I see! You're poking around in my things without permission!"

"I just picked up the magazine to have something to read while I waited for you, and it fell out," Stephie says defensively.

"Give that to me!" Vera commands.

Stephie hands her the picture. Slowly, Vera tears it to shreds.

"So now we can forget it," she says.

Stephie doesn't believe her ears.

"Do you think it will disappear just because we pretend it never existed?"

"This is none of your business," says Vera. "You'd never understand, anyway. You've lost a lot, but you still can't know what it's like never to have had anything."

"What kind of friendship do we have if you lie and keep things from me?" Stephie asks. "Don't you trust me?"

"I trust you more than anyone," Vera says softly. "But not completely. Not even you."

"How could you have let him take that kind of picture? Why, Vera?"

"There were worse poses," Vera tells her. "Where you can see even more of me. But I burned those."

She sinks onto the bed and covers her face with her hands. They are both silent for a while. When Vera looks back up, her expression is different, as if a mask had fallen away.

"He made me," she says. "Step by step. First he took a whole lot of pictures when I was dressed. He told me to smile and look one direction or the other, pull my hair forward across my shoulders, make kissing lips. Then he asked me if I would undo one or two buttons on my blouse. He said it was nice to see a little flesh at the neckline. I didn't think that sounded bad. He took a few pictures, then walked over and unbuttoned two more buttons, pulling my blouse down over my shoulders."

She goes quiet once more, takes a deep breath.

"Then he said my bra didn't look very nice and I should take it off. I didn't want to, but he said that if there was going to be any point in photographing me, it had to be a full series of shots. And he'd already wasted a whole roll on me, he said. So I did it, and once I had removed my bra, nothing seemed to matter anymore."

"Wasn't it awful?" Stephie asks. "Posing like that in front of him and his camera?"

Vera shakes her head slowly. "Not right then," she says. "Not at all, actually. He told me how pretty I was, the prettiest girl he'd photographed in ages. He said almost all the big movie stars in America had let someone take nude pictures of them before they got famous. He just talked and talked and . . ."

She goes quiet.

"And . . . ?"

"It was like he was touching me with his words," Vera tells her. "Though he used his hands, too, of course, coming over and telling me how to stand or lie. But it was his words . . . No one had ever said things like that to me before. I liked it, Stephie. I liked it!"

"Does Rikard know?"

"Are you out of your mind? He'd kill me if he found out. And he would definitely break off the engagement."

"Do you really think so?" Stephie asks. "It doesn't have anything to do with the two of you and the baby."

"Oh, yes, it does," says Vera.

"What do you mean?"

"I don't know whose baby it is. His or the photographer's."

"Vera!"

Vera grimaces. "I told you Rikard would kill me if he found out."

"Did he make you do it?"

"In a way," Vera replies. "Not by force, but I felt like I couldn't refuse."

"Why not?"

"When he'd shot three rolls, he said he was done. I started to get dressed, but then he said we weren't finished yet. 'Do you think I do this kind of thing for free?' he asked me. 'Three rolls of film and a whole afternoon's work!'

"I had some money on me, but when I pulled it out he just laughed and said money wasn't what he had in mind. He came over and kissed me and started touching my breasts. I said no and tried to pull away, but he said all the girls he photographed went to bed with him afterward. It was part of the procedure. 'If you don't, I'll burn up the film. And how are you going to get famous then?' I didn't know what to do. I thought maybe it wasn't wrong."

"Oh, Vera," says Stephie. "Vera, Vera."

She reaches out a hand and takes Vera's, holding it tight.

"I was so scared I would get pregnant," says Vera. "I thought, *Well, if I am, I have to find the kid a different father.* Rikard had been after me for a long time, and I had let him kiss me after walking me home now and then. He was kind and decent. A future engineer. But I had to hurry him, so the timing would be more or less right."

Stephie remembers that night in the cabin. The creaking mattress and Vera's giggles.

"You must've thought I was awful," says Vera. "But it really was the first—no, I mean the second—time for me. And I like him, really I do. You won't tell him, will you? You've got to promise."

Stephie is quiet for a bit. Vera is asking her to make a pretty big promise. To be party to a lie, a huge lie that will have an impact on the lives of three people. Rikard will spend his whole life sure he is the father of Vera's child, and the child will feel certain that Rikard is his or her papa.

But it may be true. The child may be Rikard's. And he cares about Vera, enough to marry her.

"Yes," Stephie says finally. "I promise, if that's what you really want. But if it were me, I wouldn't have done it."

"I know," says Vera. "But I'm not you."

28

The next day when Aunt Märta comes home, she tells Stephie that she has been to a meeting with the pastor and that there will be no collection taken up for the benefit of Stephie's parents. Instead, the congregation will pray for them and all the other victims of the war at the prayer meeting that Saturday afternoon.

"Pray for them?" Stephie spits out the words as if they were disgusting food. "They don't need our prayers. They need food and warm clothes!"

"We all need prayers," Aunt Märta placates her.

"What kind of prayers will these be?" Stephie asks. "For Jesus Christ to come back to earth and make five loaves and two fishes be enough for all the Jews in Theresienstadt?"

"That's quite enough," Aunt Märta says sternly. "No blasphemy, young lady!"

"They didn't listen to me," says Stephie. "They didn't understand at all. Aunt Märta, didn't you hear them at that meeting?"

"Yes, I did," says Aunt Märta. "I heard them, and I grieve the fact that there is so much hardness of heart among people who ought to know what love of one's fellow man implies. But we must display patience and humility in the face of God and of mankind."

Stephie doesn't answer. No one who knows Aunt Märta could possibly claim that patience and humility are her strong suits. But perhaps she is always struggling to be better at them herself, struggling to be the way her religion prescribes that she ought to be.

~

On Saturday, Stephie, in a freshly ironed dress, sits next to Aunt Märta in the house of worship. Nellie's there, too, with her tightly pulled braids and a scornful expression on her face.

"Let us pray," the pastor says, clasping those huge hands of his.

The congregation stands. There is the rustle of stiff dresses, the uneasy trampling of feet, a prayer book falling to the floor.

"I would like the Steiner girls to come forward," says the pastor.

Stephie is unable to move. She holds tightly to the back of the pew in front of her. Her throat constricts. Her heart throbs. Her eyes look straight ahead, but she senses Nellie not moving, either.

"Please come forward," the pastor repeats.

Aunt Märta nudges Stephie, as if she thinks Stephie didn't hear or was too bashful to step up.

"No," Stephie hisses out of the corner of her mouth.

The pastor looks bewildered.

"Let us pray," he repeats. "For all those who suffer because of the war, all those who have lost house and home . . ."

Stephie gets up. But she doesn't join the pastor at the front of the room. Upright as a ramrod, and without looking right or left, she walks out of the church.

∼

In the kitchen, she finds Uncle Evert. He asks no questions, says nothing about her coming home alone.

"There you are" is all he says. "I'm glad you're here. I was thinking of going out in the rowboat for a while. It's such a nice day. Won't you come along?"

Stephie nods eagerly. "I'll just get changed."

She lays out her dress on the kitchen settle, planning to hang it back in the little passage by the food cellar when she gets back. She pulls on an old skirt and blouse, and quickly ties her shoes.

Janice is lying on her stomach in the sun on the dock in nothing but a pair of shorts and a halter top. She's reading as usual, her eyes shaded by that big sun hat of hers.

When she hears footsteps, she sits up. Her hat falls off and her frizzy head of hair looks like a halo around her head. Squinting up at the sun, she smiles.

"Hedvig's gone into town," she tells Stephie. "She had some errands to do, but I promised to tell you she'll be back this evening, so there will be lessons as usual tomorrow morning."

Uncle Evert pulls the boat over. Stephie notices how hard he tries not to look at Janice. She wonders what he thinks about when he sees such a beautiful woman. What does he think about Janice's exposed, sun-warmed skin, her pretty hair, her long, lazing dancer's legs?

Suddenly, Stephie feels angry with Janice. Why doesn't she cover up? And if she wants to sunbathe practically naked, she could at least go farther from the house.

Janice seems to read her thoughts, because she gets up and pulls the towel she's been lying on around her shoulders. But perhaps she does so only because the sun's suddenly gone behind a little cloud.

"Going for a spin in the boat?" Janice asks.

"Yes," Stephie answers curtly.

She's afraid Janice is going to ask if she can come along. She wants this time alone with Uncle Evert.

"Coming, Stephie?" Uncle Evert asks.

"Right away!"

❦

Stephie's sitting in the stern, listening to the creaking of the oars in the wooden oarlocks, the heavy splash as the blades hit the surface, the clucking of the water against the sides of the boat. Those rhythmic sounds make her feel calmer, but her chest is still tight.

"Have you heard from your parents again?"

Uncle Evert rests on the oars and searches Stephie's face.

"No," Stephie replies. "It's been weeks."

"You mustn't lose hope," says Uncle Evert. "I know how upsetting it is, but you mustn't lose hope. The war is going to end. The Allies are already in Italy. It may all be over in a matter of months now. In the long run, evil will not be the victor. Do you believe me?"

Stephie nods.

"Bear up," says Uncle Evert. "No matter how hard it may be, we must bear up. And the weight of the entire world isn't on your shoulders, thank goodness, since they are quite small."

He pulls on one oar to straighten the rowboat's drifting course.

"Your turn to row," he says.

They change seats. Stephie rows with long, powerful strokes, as Uncle Evert has taught her. It feels good to be exerting herself, putting in some effort, using her arms. Her lungs fill with air. She breathes more easily, feels stronger.

Yes, she will bear up. She will!

29

The following day is the first sunny Sunday of August, so May and her family finally come to visit. All seven children are here, as well as May's mother, panting in the heat.

"Gustav didn't come along in the end," Mrs. Karlsson says. "My husband is not too keen on sun and swimming. He's happier in the city."

In her net bag, she has a coffee cake from the bakery in Sandarna, and although Aunt Märta usually turns up her nose at bought baked goods, she thanks May's mother politely and slices it up to go with the coffee.

Aunt Märta spent the morning in church. Stephie didn't have to go along, since she was meeting May's family when they arrived. That was a relief. She was even less eager to go to church than usual, after the previous day.

The normally quiet house is full of noise once May's brothers and sisters feel comfortable there. When Miss Björk heard that the whole Karlsson family was coming to visit, she said they were free to use the real kitchen and sitting room instead of crowding into the basement rooms. She and Janice are on a boat outing and aren't expected back until evening.

Kurre and Olle are out on the lawn kicking a soccer ball. Their loud shouts can be heard through the open window. Erik is running up and down the stairs between the hall and the bedrooms. He's never been in a home that has a staircase inside. Ninni is playing with Stephie's old teddy bear, talking to herself as she puts it to bed in a sugar crate under a piece of cloth. Britten turns the knobs on the radio, until May scolds her.

"Leave that radio alone, Britten!" May tells her. "There's enough noise in here already."

May knows, of course, that the only thing Aunt Märta allows the radio to be used for is to listen to the news and religious music. Not to mention that it's Sunday. Listening to secular music on a Sunday is even more sinful in Aunt Märta's eyes.

While they're having their coffee, Uncle Evert appears in his Sunday suit and a tie. He went to church with Aunt Märta this morning, and then stopped by the harbor to hear if there was any news.

"They've raised up the *Wolf*," he tells them. "Apparently, they're taking her right to Göteborg. I guess they'll pass this way this afternoon."

The efforts to tow the *Wolf* have been ongoing all summer. Although divers have been down to look, no one yet knows what caused the accident.

May's mother has brought a picnic, sandwiches, and cold fried eggs for herself and the children. Aunt Märta wants to treat them to a meal, but May's mother says it's out of the question.

"There are far too many of us, Mrs. Jansson. We'd eat you out of house and home! If a woman has seven children, she has to take responsibility for them herself."

⁓

After they've been for a swim and eaten, the group makes its way in procession to the harbor. Uncle Evert heads it up, with Kurre and Olle marching proudly, one on each side of him. Uncle Evert has promised to show them around the *Diana*. They'll get to go on board and look at all the fishing equipment and the instruments used to guide the boat. Erik runs eagerly on their heels. Next come May and Stephie, arm in arm, each holding the hand of one of the younger girls. Britten follows them closely, trying to get in on their conversation.

Last are Aunt Märta and Mrs. Karlsson. One tall, slim woman with a tight bun at the nape of her neck, one short and stout in a flowered summer dress with perspiration stains at the underarms. In spite of looking so different, they seem to be getting along well.

All over the island, flags fly at half-mast. Before they left home, Uncle Evert pulled their own flag halfway down. They are showing their respect for the crew of the *Wolf.* Sundays are always solemn days on the island, but today, people's faces are even graver than usual, and lots of people have kept their Sunday clothes on after having been at one of the three churches on the island.

A crowd has gathered on a little point not far from the harbor. They're waiting to see the *Wolf* as she is towed past. Uncle Evert's group stops here, in spite of Kurre and Olle's eagerness to go aboard the *Diana.*

"Take it easy," says Uncle Evert. "There's plenty of time. The boat back to town isn't until six."

Aunt Märta and May's mother sit down on the rocks. May sits down, too, with Ninni on her lap and Stephie close by. Erik and Gunnel run around. Uncle Evert recites the names of the nearby islands to Kurre and Olle.

It doesn't take long for the little convoy to appear to the northwest. There's the ship towing the *Wolf,* along with various other ships. They move in a silent formation, proceeding slowly on the way to the mouth of the harbor in Göteborg.

"They're taking her to the Eriksberg shipyard," says Kurre. "Papa says they've been preparing the big dry dock for her all week."

The people on the shore are silent as the naval ships

pass close enough that they can see the contours of the submarine clearly at the waterline.

Inside, thirty-three crewmen lie dead, many of them not much older than Stephie and May, in a coffin of steel.

Everyone stays until the convoy is out of sight behind the next island. Slowly, the solemn gathering disperses. But Stephie feels pensive.

She feels as if a gust of icy cold wind has blown through the hot summer day.

30

"Aunt Märta?"

"Yes?"

Aunt Märta looks up from the fisherman's overalls she is mending.

"I . . . ," Stephie begins. "There's something I'd like to talk to you about, Aunt Märta."

She has been putting this conversation off for days now. In spite of having made up her mind and being sure she's doing the right thing, it's still difficult to tell Aunt Märta.

"What is it?"

Aunt Märta snaps off a thread with a decisive pull.

She has to say it now. *Once you've started something, you've got to go through with it,* as Aunt Märta often says.

"Well . . . I . . ."

"My dear girl, what on earth is the matter? Has the cat got your tongue?"

Now. She's got to say it now.

"I'm going to resign from the Pentecostal congregation."

Stephie's words immediately erect a mountain between them. How can eight words take up so much space? They fill the entire room with a rumbling silence.

Aunt Märta sits perfectly still. She stares at her right hand, the one holding the needle with the dangling thread, as if she isn't sure what she had been planning to do with it.

"I'm sorry," says Stephie. "I'm terribly sorry, Aunt Märta, but I have to do it."

"Are you certain?" Aunt Märta asks, her voice dull and distant.

"Yes."

"Is it because of the fuss about the collection?"

"That's not the only reason."

"Have you lost your faith?"

I never had any to begin with, Stephie thinks but is unable to say. Her years of false Christianity cling to her stickily. She has been pretending for too long to be able to tell Aunt Märta the whole truth now.

"Yes."

"Will you pray with me for its return?"

Aunt Märta rises from her chair. The overalls slip to

the floor. She falls to her knees on the hard kitchen floor and clasps her hands.

"Dear Jesus," she prays. "See to our sister who wanders in darkness. Show her Your light . . ."

Aunt Märta's scraggy hand reaches out for Stephie's. She pulls it, not hard but in a grip that is impossible to resist. Stephie falls to her knees beside her.

". . . and open her heart to Your love . . ."

She doesn't want Jesus' love. But does that mean she will have to lose Aunt Märta's?

Aunt Märta's love. She has never thought in those terms before. That Aunt Märta loves her.

She remembers the first time she saw Aunt Märta. It was at Auntie Alma's. She seemed so cold, Stephie thought she must have a film of ice around her. She remembers the time Aunt Märta slapped her face on the stairs, and the time she punished her for having taken Auntie Alma's china dog. She also recalls the joy she felt the time Aunt Märta defended her and called her "my girl."

Mamma and Papa are so far away. Aunt Märta and Uncle Evert are all she has. Isn't it worth accepting Jesus, too, in the bargain?

". . . still her uneasy heart," Aunt Märta prays.

Still her uneasy heart. Summer vacation will be over soon, and Stephie hasn't heard from Mamma and Papa once. Where are they? Are they still in Theresienstadt? Or are they *abgereist,* departed, that blurry word Judith used but refused to explain?

You have betrayed your own people, Judith had said. In that case, she has also betrayed Mamma and Papa.

She ought to have done more. She ought not to have given up without getting them permits to come to Sweden. If only she hadn't been so young when she'd gotten here! Now that she's nearly grown up, it's too late. Mamma and Papa wouldn't be released from the camp even if Sweden agreed to have them.

"Can't you pray?" Aunt Märta asks, her hand grazing Stephie's shoulder. "Try!"

"God," says Stephie, "if you exist, God, give me my mamma and papa back!" Tears run down her cheeks. "Mamma!" she cries. "I want my mamma here."

⁊

Later, when Aunt Märta has wrapped Stephie in a blanket, led her to the kitchen settle, and given her a cup of hot honey water to drink, they sit silently as the August evening turns to night.

Aunt Märta stirs her coffee.

"I know," she says, "that I cannot replace your mother. But I also want you to know that whatever happens, you will always have a home here, with me and Evert."

"I'm sorry," says Stephie. "I'm sorry to be ungrateful. But I cannot change my mind."

"There's no need to apologize."

Aunt Märta takes a swallow from her cup.

"I don't want you to imagine," she says slowly, "that

I haven't wondered whether we did the right thing, Alma and I. Wondered if it was wrong to have you and Nellie baptized and taken up as members of the congregation. Perhaps we should have waited. But I thought Jesus would be a comfort to you, as he was to me in my hour of greatest need."

She sits silently again.

"When Anna-Lisa died?" Stephie asks in a whisper.

This is the first time she has ever said Anna-Lisa's name in Aunt Märta's presence. She has only talked to Auntie Alma about Aunt Märta and Uncle Evert's daughter, who died of tuberculosis at the age of twelve. And Uncle Evert knows that Stephie knows that the red sled they gave her the first winter on the island had belonged to Anna-Lisa. But in all these years, Aunt Märta has never said a word about her child who died, and Stephie has yielded to her silence.

"That's right," says Aunt Märta. "When Anna-Lisa died, I don't think I could have gone on living if I hadn't had my faith. And then later, you came along."

That night, Stephie dreams about Mamma. She's in her Queen of the Night costume, a shiny black velvet dress, and her face is as pale as the moon. Stephie can see that she's singing, but she cannot hear a word.

31

"No, nothing today, either."

Miss Holm looks regretfully at Stephie over the rims of her gold-framed glasses.

"But I'm sure you'll hear tomorrow," the postmistress continues quickly.

Stephie nods in agreement. Miss Holm means well. Still, her attempts at encouragement are nothing but empty phrases. She knows no more than Stephie about why the cards from Mamma and Papa have stopped arriving.

Stephie puts her letter on the counter. Miss Holm stamps it, postmarks it, and accepts Stephie's two ten-öre coins.

"Stop by again tomorrow. I'm sure there will be something for you."

Nellie and her summer friend, Maud, are sitting on the stone wall outside the shop by the post office, eating caramels from a big bag.

"Want one?" Maud asks, holding out the bag to Stephie.

Stephie puts a caramel in her mouth. It's sticky and sweet.

"Have another," Maud offers.

Stephie shakes her head.

"There wasn't a card today, either," she tells Nellie.

"All right, then." Nellie's tone is brusque.

"Are you almost like orphans?" Maud asks. "That's what Nellie says."

"No, we're not," Stephie hisses. "It's just that our parents can't come to Sweden until the war is over. Don't talk so much foolishness, Nellie!"

I didn't say we *are* orphans," Nellie says defensively. "I just said that when we first came, it was almost like the story in that book . . ." She turns to Maud. "The one you lent me. What was it called again?"

"Anne of Green Gables," says Maud.

Aha, Stephie thinks, *so Nellie borrows books from Maud. That's a good thing.* Otherwise, Nellie isn't particularly interested in reading, and she certainly never reads any German books nowadays. Her school grades are only average. She'll never get a scholarship in two years, when she finishes compulsory school. Stephie can only hope that the war will be over by then and Nellie will be able to continue her education anyway.

Maud whispers something to Nellie, and both girls giggle.

"Ask her!" says Maud, nudging Nellie with her elbow.

"No," says Nellie. "You ask her."

"No, you do it."

"Who's the father of Vera's baby?" Nellie asks.

Vera's almost five months pregnant now, and there's no hiding her stomach any longer.

"Her fiancé, of course," Stephie replies.

"What's his name?"

"Rikard."

"Do you know him?"

"No," says Stephie, "I've met him, but I can't say I know him."

"Why aren't they married?" asks Maud. "You're supposed to be married before you have babies."

"It's a sin," says Nellie. "What Vera did." She pinches her lips like one of the ladies at the Pentecostal church. "A siiiin," she repeats.

"A siiiin," Maud echoes with a giggle.

"Auntie Alma says you're not a Christian anymore, Stephie," says Nellie. "Is it true?"

"Yes," Stephie answers. "I've resigned from the congregation."

"Jesus will be upset," says Nellie. "Auntie Alma says so."

"Jesus can't be upset," Maud tells her. "He's dead." She laughs.

Nellie looks anxious, but then she joins in with a high-pitched, exaggerated laugh.

Stephie doesn't join in. Why is Nellie so desperately eager to please Maud?

If she hadn't been making the very same prediction every day for weeks now, one might think Miss Holm could predict the future.

"Here it is at last!" she cries out triumphantly the next day as she extends a postcard to Stephie.

Stephie's excitement about reading the card right away is offset by the knowledge that if she reads it in the post office, Miss Holm won't let her leave until she hears exactly what it says. Trying to appear offhanded, she puts the card in her pocket.

"Thank you very much."

Miss Holm looks disappointed.

Stephie goes out onto the steps. As she's pulling out the card, she hears a commotion. A man shouts. A girl screams.

"No! No! Let me go!"

The voices are coming from the open door to the shop close by the post office. Stephie turns in that direction and sees Maud rushing down the shop steps as if shot out of a cannon.

But she wasn't the one shouting. It was Nellie.

At a run, Stephie crosses the graveled yard between the post office and the shop, and up the five steps. It takes a fraction of a second for her eyes to adjust from the blinding sunshine outside to the dim light of the shop.

The shopkeeper is standing in the middle of the floor, his face scarlet with anger. He is holding Nellie tightly by her black braids. Nellie is sobbing hysterically. Caramels and other candies are all over the floor. Sylvia is standing on the stairs. She gives Stephie a scornful smile.

Behind Stephie, a couple of ladies peek in through the open door.

"What's going on?" Stephie cries. "Let her go!"

"You'd like that, wouldn't you?" the shopkeeper roars. "But I don't let thieves off so easily."

"My sister is no thief!"

The shopkeeper gestures at the floor with his free hand.

"Oh, no? Just look at what she stole while her friend lured me into the stockroom to get her something!"

The ladies have pushed past Stephie. They're looking at each other and muttering. The shopkeeper enjoys having an audience.

"Just look! Just look what this little Jew brat has done!"

"Don't tell Auntie Alma!" Nellie sniffles. "Please, please don't say anything to Auntie Alma. I'll pay for every single piece."

"Sylvia just happened to come downstairs," the shopkeeper says to his customers, "and she saw this little rat standing there, stealing from the candy jars. The other girl's the daughter of one of the summer guests. She was keeping guard to see when I came back."

Sylvia raises her well-plucked eyebrows.

"I'm sure it wasn't the first time," she says. "It was just a lucky coincidence that I happened to be coming down."

"But it *was* the first time!" Nellie cries. "And I'll never do it again, just as long as Auntie Alma doesn't find out."

"Not a chance," says the shopkeeper. "Don't you go getting any ideas. I'm most certainly going to tell Mrs. Lindberg what you get yourself into when you take in kids from foreign countries. Sylvia, you mind the shop while I'm gone."

Still holding Nellie tightly by the braids, the shopkeeper marches out the door, down the steps, across the graveled yard, and down the street in the direction of Auntie Alma's house.

"Let her walk on her own," Stephie pleads. "The least you could do is to let her walk on her own."

"So she can run off and hide?" asks the shopkeeper.

"Not on my watch. She deserves a good licking, and I intend to see that she gets one."

Stephie follows them. What else can she do? The card is in her skirt pocket, forgotten. Her cheeks burn with shame. Her sister is a thief.

32

Although it's not far from the shop to Auntie Alma's, it feels as if they walk for an eternity. Nellie stumbles forward, the shopkeeper's big hand on her neck. Stephie pushes her bike behind them, looking straight down into the gray, dusty road so as not to have to face the curious gazes of the people they pass.

At last they arrive. Maud's mother is sitting in the garden with a friend. No one else is in sight.

"No, Mrs. Lindberg isn't at home," Maud's mother tells him. "She's gone to the next island over to visit a relative who's ill. She took the two little ones with her. I've promised to make dinner for Nellie. Is something wrong? Why are you holding her like that?"

To Stephie's surprise, the shopkeeper doesn't answer.

been your friend since your first day of
d when Maud goes back to Göteborg this
vill still be here, where you live."

ts up. She puts the suitcase back in the crawl

u stay?" she asks. "Until Auntie Alma gets

nods. "Of course I will."

age to tell Auntie Alma the whole story be-
hopkeeper calls. Auntie Alma is angry and
lie ask for forgiveness. First Auntie Alma's,
's, on her knees. Stephie looks away.
n Auntie Alma hears how the shopkeeper be-
is just as angry with him, and says Nellie cer-
going to be humiliated in front of that man.
ng a child that way! It's not Christian," she

about Maud?" Stephie asks. "Auntie Alma,
going to have a word with her mother?"
Alma considers. "I'm not really sure."
d been Sonja," Stephie says, "you would have
er mother right away."
" says Auntie Alma. "But this is another mat-
re different."
se they're summer guests?"
husband's a professor," Auntie Alma tells

He doesn't ask where Maud is, either. He just lets Nellie go.

"Don't think you're going to get off scot-free," he mutters to her. "I'll be calling Mrs. Lindberg tonight."

The minute he lets go of Nellie, she rushes inside. Not down to the basement rooms where she, Auntie Alma, Uncle Sigurd, Elsa, and John are living during the summer, but through the veranda door and straight up the stairs to the rooms the summer tenants are renting. Stephie says a few words of apology to Maud's mother and follows her sister.

She finds Nellie in the crawl space under the stairs to the attic. At first, Stephie thinks she's crept in there to hide, like an injured animal, until she sees that Nellie is looking for something. From behind some other things, she pulls out a little suitcase.

Stephie recognizes it. It's the one Nellie had when they arrived on the island. She has an identical one herself. It has moved with her from Vienna to the island, from the island to the apartment of the doctor's family in Göteborg, from there to Miss Björk's, and finally to Sandarna. Now it's in the attic storage space in May's family's apartment building.

Nellie's suitcase, though, has probably been put away for four years. She hasn't moved since they came to Sweden.

"What do you need your suitcase for?" Stephie asks.

"You can't really think Auntie Alma will still want me here when she finds out about this?"

"Don't be silly. Of course she will."

"What do you know?" asks Nellie. "And maybe I don't want to stay here, either."

"Where were you planning on going, then?"

Nellie shrugs. She looks determined, but Stephie sees a little quiver in her bottom lip that she recognizes from when Nellie was little and about to burst into tears.

"Nellie," Stephie tells her, "Auntie Alma is going to be angry, but she's not going to throw you out. I'm absolutely sure. You would be sure, too, if you thought it through. I've done worse things, you know, without Aunt Märta showing me the door, and you know how strict she is."

Nellie looks incredulous. "You have?"

"Sure," says Stephie. "I took Auntie Alma's china dog, don't you remember? And I went to the movies even though we aren't allowed to."

"You had to apologize in church," says Nellie.

"Right."

"Do you think I'll have to apologize, too?"

"Maybe."

Nellie sits down on her small suitcase, chin in hand. Her black braids reach almost all the way to the floor.

She sat that very same way four years ago in the railway station in Göteborg while they were waiting for someone to come and take charge of them.

Stephie sits down on the bottom step of the attic stairs.

"Why did you do it?" she asks.

Nellie sighs. "I can'

"Why not?"

Maud, Stephie thin

"Did Maud put you

Nellie starts to sniff

"Tell me," says Step

"She said it was my

"She's always got mon

I never have any. Wh

money, she said it was

handfuls of sweets in t

the shopkeeper to go i

take the candy and run

"Then it's just as mu

"If not more."

"What difference do

terly. "Her mamma nev

if something breaks or g

"So why do you pla

friends. Like Sonja."

"She likes me," says N

"Doesn't Sonja?"

"Well, I guess so. But

one to come up with thi

about anything but her

cousins and all the peop

and who she's going to n

"But she's your friend

"So what?"

"Mind your manners!" Auntie Alma snaps. "Is that the kind of thing you learn at grammar school? How to be rude about people of a better class?"

"Better? Having money and fancy positions doesn't make people better!"

"That's quite enough," says Auntie Alma.

At that very moment, Maud's mother calls down from upstairs that there's a phone call for Mrs. Lindberg. Auntie Alma goes to take it.

"You shouldn't have brought that up," says Nellie. "I don't want her talking to Maud's mother, either. But I'm going to play with Sonja tomorrow."

≈∫

Not until Stephie's on her way home does she remember the card in her pocket. But it's getting dark out now. There isn't enough light for her to read it.

Suddenly she's in a hurry. She has to find out what that little rectangle of stiff, yellowish cardboard says.

Her bike light sheds a diffuse light on the road in front of her. But when she stops pedaling, the generator stops working, too, and the light fades.

She tries spinning the front wheel with one hand while holding the card in front of the light with the other. It's impossible. Not enough friction. She'll have to wait until she gets home.

Stephie pedals as fast as she can, leans the bike against the house, and pulls the card out of her pocket again.

Standing outside the basement kitchen window, she reads.

Theresienstadt, 3 July 1943

Dearest Stephie!
  Forgive me, I've not been able to write until now. Mamma died of typhus on June 17. Endless grief. Be gentle as you can when you tell Nellie.

Your Papa

33

Only thirty words.

Thirty words as heavy as the boulders down by the shore. Dark, immovable. A weight pressing Stephie down to the ground and threatening to suffocate her.

She was in a rush a few minutes ago; now she feels paralyzed. Slowly, the hand holding the card sinks down and remains slack at her side. Her feet feel as if they were cemented in the gravel.

Her legs won't carry her. Everything that held her upright before, every bone in her body, all her muscles and cartilage, seem to have dissolved. Her body is a quivering mass, like one of those horrid jellyfish down by the sea.

She wants to scream, but she has no voice, either. All that comes across her lips is a soft moan.

She falls into a black hole. A black vacuum that sucks her into a vortex of misery.

Aunt Märta opens the cellar door and pops her head out.

"Stephie? Stephie, is that you? Why don't you come inside?" And then, in a voice full of concern, "Are you all right? Why are you lying there? Are you sick?"

❧

It takes a long time for Stephie to be able to speak. By then, Aunt Märta has helped her up and led her gently to the kitchen settle. She sits there with her arms around Stephie, cradling Stephie's dark head against her chest.

"My little girl, my dear little girl," she murmurs.

Although Stephie hasn't said a word, and although Aunt Märta cannot read the German text on the card, Stephie knows that Aunt Märta knows. That she understands.

Everything hurts. Her clothes are rubbing against her body as if she were sunburned. The light from the ceiling lamp is burning in her eyes. Even when she shuts them, she sees little bolts of lightning inside her eyelids.

Slowly, she runs her tongue around the inside of her mouth. It feels like a shapeless lump.

"Aunt Märta . . . could you please turn off the light?"

Aunt Märta lights the stump of a candle and turns off the electric light.

"Is that better?"

"Yes, thank you."

Stephie lowers herself so that she is lying down on the settle. She shuts her eyes again. Lies absolutely still.

The bolts of lightning are gone now. Instead, images streak by. Dreamlike images of Mamma as Queen of the Night, singing wordlessly. Mamma in a hospital bed. Mamma at the train station the day they were parted, her bright red lips a gaping wound.

She should never have left. She should have stayed with Mamma and Papa. Now it's too late to do anything.

This is the darkest night, the longest. Although it's still summer, dawn never seems to come. Rain-heavy clouds hang darkly over the sea.

For that whole long night, Aunt Märta sits on a chair beside the kitchen settle, while Stephie twists and turns in uneasy sleep. Now and then, she touches Stephie's cheek lightly, as she did that very first night she had a little girl in her house again after all those childless years.

The dawn brings the rain. Upstairs, where Miss Björk and Janice are asleep in their beds, the heavy drops patter against the roof. In the basement, the rain swishes against the windowpanes. Aunt Märta blows out the candle and starts the morning pot of coffee.

Stephie wakes up with a burning emptiness in her chest.

Dead. Mamma is dead.

On the chair where Aunt Märta had been sitting, she finds Miss Björk.

"Mrs. Jansson is getting a little rest," she says.

Never, in all the years she has known her, has Stephie seen Aunt Märta lie down to rest during the day. Neither exhaustion nor knee pain have stopped her from being active, dawn to dusk. The only rest she has ever allowed herself was to sit down for a cup of coffee in the morning and another midafternoon.

Miss Björk notices Stephie's worried look.

"Don't be frightened," she says. "She isn't ill. But I had the impression she'd been up all night."

Stephie remembers the voice talking to her in the semidarkness, the hand stroking her cheek.

"All night," she murmurs. "Did she sit here all night?"

Miss Björk nods. "No words can convey how sorry I am for your loss, Stephanie. And for your sister's."

Nellie. *Be as gentle as you can when you tell Nellie.*

"She doesn't know yet?" Miss Björk asks, her voice soft and sympathetic.

"No. I'm going to have to tell her."

"If you'd like, I could phone her foster mother. And she can tell Nellie."

Stephie shakes her head. "No, I have to do it myself."

"I thought that was what you'd say."

Miss Björk keeps a discreet distance while Stephie gets up and dresses. Everything takes so long. Do the buttons on her blouse usually slip between her fingers? Is it always so hard to buckle her sandals?

"Would you like me to come along?"

"Thank you for offering, but I'll go alone."

"All right. You'd better have some coffee and a sandwich first, though, don't you think? We don't want you passing out again, do we?"

Actually, she is hungry. Distantly she recalls that neither she nor Nellie had any dinner yesterday. Neither of them felt like sitting at the table with Maud and her family.

Miss Björk pours Stephie a cup of coffee and puts butter, cheese, and bread on the table.

Mamma always served them breakfast back in Vienna, before they left for school. Fresh bread from the bakery and hot chocolate. That was the only meal she prepared herself. Otherwise, the kitchen was the cook's territory.

"In the mornings, I want to look after my girls," Mamma used to say.

She was different in the mornings. Without lipstick and with her black hair loose over her shoulders, she looked like a young girl.

"No one can take your memories away from you," says Miss Björk.

Stephie is so startled she spills a little coffee into her saucer.

211

"What do you mean?"

"No one can take your memories away from you," Hedvig Björk repeats. "They are part of you. Your mother will stay alive inside you."

Those words release a tightness in Stephie's chest, and her tears flow like a flood that she feels in her whole body.

"Mamma!" she sobs. "Mamma! Mamma! Why couldn't I have been there with you?"

34

When Aunt Märta comes in, she tells Stephie she has spoken to Auntie Alma.

"I asked her to send Nellie over," she says. "I thought you'd want to tell her yourself. Nellie can spend the night if she wants to."

Stephie sits on the front steps, waiting for Nellie. It has stopped raining and the sun is looking out from between clouds. The steps are already dry.

Be as gentle as you can when you tell Nellie.

It's a beautiful day. The sky is blue and quickly clears so that soon there are just a few white, airy clouds. The sun reflects brightly off the sea. A gentle wind caresses Stephie's face. *How can anything be so pretty when Mamma is dead?*

Nellie leans her bike up against the house.

"What is it?" she asks. "Auntie Alma said you had something important to tell me."

"Come along," says Stephie. "Let's go sit on the dock."

"But what is it?" Nellie nags.

Stephie doesn't answer. She walks ahead onto the dock, and Nellie follows. Not until they are sitting next to each other on the edge does Stephie speak.

"Do you remember the nursery we shared at home in Vienna?" she asks. "Before we had to move?"

Nellie thinks.

"Yes," she says after a while. "We had white beds. Yours was on one side of the room and mine on the other."

"Do you remember how Mamma used to tuck us in at bedtime?"

"Yes."

"What do you remember?"

"That she smelled good. She used to sing for us before turning out the lights."

"This one?"

Stephie starts humming one of Mamma's lullabies.

"Yes, I remember that one. She even taught me to play it on the piano when I got a little bigger."

"Right," Stephie tells her. "You were really good at the piano even when you were very young. You're musical, just like Mamma. You inherited that from her."

Nellie looks suspiciously at Stephie. "What's with you today?"

Stephie bites her lip. A minute ago, she thought she had broken through Nellie's prickly shell. But this is going to be more difficult than she imagined.

"You asked me once," she goes on, "if I thought Mamma and Papa were thinking of us. It was on New Year's Eve. Do you remember my answer?"

"No," says Nellie.

"I told you that wherever they are and whatever they're doing, I'm sure they're thinking about us."

"But I don't think about them often enough? Is that what you're getting at?" Nellie gets up. "If that's what you're after, I'm not going to sit here and listen to you. All you want to do is to make me feel guilty."

Stephie's losing her. She's got to tell Nellie now.

"Wait," she says. "I've still got something to tell you."

"What?"

"Sit back down."

Nellie does, reluctantly.

"Do you remember when Mamma got sick, the second winter after we left? She got pneumonia right when she and Papa were supposed to be leaving for America."

"Of course," says Nellie. "Of course I remember."

"Mamma got sick again," Stephie tells her. "In the camp. At Theresienstadt."

"Oh?"

215

"She got seriously ill," Stephie continues. "Typhus. I don't know much about it, though."

"But Papa can take care of her, right?"

Now Stephie can clearly hear Nellie's concern.

"Nellie," says Stephie. "Mamma is dead."

For an instant, there is total silence. Neither of them moves a muscle.

Then a seagull screeches overhead. Nellie is on her feet again.

"You liar!" she cries. "She's not dead! You're just making that up to punish me. You think you do everything right, and I'm stupid and mean. You liar!"

The tears stream from her eyes. Stephie stands, and Nellie pounds her with her fists.

"Liar! Liar!" she screams.

Stephie takes Nellie by the wrists and holds her still. Nellie struggles, but eventually gives up. Her body is quaking with sobs. Stephie puts her arms around her, holding her tight.

"It's my fault," Nellie sobs. "It's my fault she's dead."

"Why on earth would it be your fault?"

"For wishing I was Aunt Alma and Uncle Sigurd's own child. I didn't want any other mother than Auntie Alma."

"Listen to me now, Nellie," says Stephie. "Nothing is your fault. We were sent here like packages with address labels around our necks. That wasn't our fault, and it wasn't Mamma and Papa's fault, either. You were now; there isn't much time left before the

s so kind to her. Aunt Märta looks after her
er favorite meals. Miss Björk encourages
ice tries to make her laugh. Uncle Evert
and takes her out in the little rowboat. He
much, but listening to the rhythm of the
king into his eyes calms her.
gs over a tin cup with the very first black-
e summer.
ur spot," she tells Stephie.
ms happy, in spite of not being able to go
job in Göteborg when summer is over. Her
oesn't want a housemaid who's expecting,
hasn't yet managed to arrange an apartment
o live in once they're married.
s will all work out," Vera says, stroking her
What do you think it's going to be, a boy or

," says Stephie.
e so," says Vera. "Though it's probably easier
oy."
e has no idea how May hears the news, but
eek or so, she gets a long letter. May writes how
e feels for Stephie, and how much she wishes she
elp. She sends greetings from her whole family,
rawing from Gunnel, with Stephie as a princess.
ie, in turn, writes to Papa. She has never had so

so little. I promised I would take care of you, but I couldn't."

"The first evening here," Nellie whispers. "When you left with Aunt Märta. I thought you were never coming back."

"I had no choice. I had to go."

"If nobody ever has any choice," Nellie asks her, "then whose fault is it?"

35

The days pass. The first raging grief slides into a more muffled sorrow. Stephie misses Mamma all the time, and sometimes she cries.

"Let her cry," she hears Miss Björk tell Aunt Märta. "It eases the grief. I know. I lost my mother when I was her age."

"I should never have come to Sweden," Stephie says, weeping. "I should have been there."

"That's not true," says Miss Björk firmly.

"Yes, it is. I ought to have been there, with Mamma."

"And if you had died, too? Do you think it would have been better for her to know that? Or for your papa? Believe me, Stephanie, as long as your mother was alive, she was grateful that you and Nellie were in good hands. And papa now? Knowi

Papa. Oh, how l

"I don't know y from all you've tol of."

"What's that?"

"That whatever ha give up. You are here reason is for you to g of your life."

Stephie looks up and rious gaze. Stephie kno There are fewer than t that will determine whe of high school. It all feels has anything to do with

"I don't know if I can d

"But I know you can," We'll start studying aga right?"

"All right."

"Your mamma would be Björk.

Gradually, life's daily routines Stephie goes upstairs to study

to work hard tests.

Everyone i and makes her, and Jar comes home doesn't say oars and lo

Vera brin berries of t

"From o

Vera see back to he mistress and Rikar for them

"Thing tummy. a girl?"

"A girl

"I ho to be a

Steph after a sorry sh could h and a

Step

much trouble formulating a letter. She has to start over and over again. The fountain pen trembles in her hand. But finally she finds the words.

> *Dearest Papa,*
> *I miss you both so dreadfully. Mamma, dead, and you, out of reach. I love both of you more than anything in the world. But I know you did the right thing in sending us here. I am fortunate, having people who care about me. And the war will end, someday. And we will be reunited.*
>
> *Love,*
> *Stephie*

She mails the letter.
It comes back.
Abgereist, says the stamp on the envelope.
Departed? Departed for where?

❧

The entrance examinations for high school take two days. Stephie goes to Göteborg with Miss Björk and Janice, whose summer vacation is now over. Miss Björk has to prepare for her fall classes, and Janice is starting rehearsals at the opera house.

The tests go well. Stephie feels well prepared. The

night between the two test days, Stephie sleeps in her bed at May's. After the tests, she'll return to the island for the last week of her summer vacation.

It's good to see May again, and the rest of her family, too. May's mother gives her a hug and kisses both her cheeks, and Gunnel comes over and sits on Stephie's lap. That night, Stephie and May lie whispering for a long time before they fall asleep.

The second day, Stephie finishes by early afternoon. She could take the three o'clock boat to the island, but she decides to wait and leave that evening instead. There is one thing she needs to do before going back.

At four-thirty, she rings the bell of the Jewish Children's Home. Susie, the girl with the sulky face, opens the door. At first, she doesn't recognize Stephie, but after a moment, she tells her to come in.

"Is Judith here?" Stephie asks.

"No, she's not back from work yet. You can wait in the dayroom."

Stephie sits down on a hard chair. She hears girls talking to each other, somewhere else in the building. A tall girl comes in to get a book and nods to Stephie.

"Are you looking for someone?" the girl asks.

"Yes, Judith."

"Oh, are you her classmate from Vienna? The one who lives on an island?"

"Yes, I am," says Stephie, wondering what Judith has been saying about her. But the girl gives her a friendly smile before leaving with the book under her arm.

Twenty minutes later, Judith finally arrives.

"Judith, you've got a visitor!" she hears Susie shout.

Stephie rises from the armchair just as Judith steps in the doorway, looking surprised.

"Stephie! What are you doing here?"

I shouldn't have come, Stephie thinks. *She doesn't want to see me.*

But Judith walks into the room and takes one of Stephie's hand in both of hers. Her eyes are bright.

"I'm so glad to see you! I behaved very foolishly. Can you forgive me?"

"It doesn't matter," says Stephie. "You were right, too, in a way. In fact, I resigned from the church congregation."

"You did? Oh, I'm so glad you aren't mad at me. You're the only person here I know from home."

"Judith," Stephie asks. "What does *abgereist* mean?"

Judith's smile vanishes. "Your parents?" she asks.

"Papa. Mamma is dead. She died in June, though I didn't hear about it until a couple of weeks ago. You do know what *abgereist* means, don't you?"

"Transported," Judith tells her. "To another camp. Probably in Poland. No letters ever arrive from there. You can't write or send packages."

"What happens there?"

"I don't know," says Judith. "No one knows for sure. All you can do is hope."

"Hope for what?"

"That the war will end. Fast, before they're all dead."

During the last vacation week on the island, the air is cooler, and the blue of the sea is a shade darker. Autumn is approaching.

On Monday, Uncle Evert takes the *Diana* out in a convoy with several fishing boats. Fishing together is safest, in case one of the boats hits a mine. That has happened several times this summer, but no one has been killed.

On Wednesday evening, the boats are already back. All but two. Two boats and their crews are missing.

"They got shot down," Uncle Evert tells Stephie. "On purpose. No one, not even the Germans, can mistake a fishing boat for a naval vessel. They're trying to frighten us. And it's working. They were so close they could surely see the name and number of every single boat. They'll get the rest of us next time."

None of the boats go out fishing again that week. There are protest meetings on the islands and in the fishing villages along the coast. The boats that were with the two that got shot down change their names and numbers. Although no one is safe in these waters anymore, the risk is greatest for boats whose crews have seen too much.

"The *Liberty*," suggests Uncle Evert. "Don't you think a name meaning 'freedom' would be good, Stephie?"

Stephie nods. "*Liberty*'s a good name.

"Or maybe . . . ," says Uncle Evert. "Wasn't your mother's name Elisabeth?"

"Yes."

"Shall we rename the boat after her?"

"Is the *Elisabeth* a good name for a boat?"

"Yes," Uncle Evert answers. "A very good name."

Stephie helps paint the new name—*Elisabeth*—in big black letters on the rounded stern. Uncle Evert paints the name of the island and the boat's number.

"We'll go out again next week," he says. "Those Germans can't get rid of us that easily. Soon it will be their turn to be afraid."

36

Stephie is standing on a cliff a couple of yards above the sea, in the hard September wind. It makes the water choppy, tearing up waves every which way and leaving a line of white foam along the shoreline.

She knows quite a lot about the sea now. Uncle Evert has taught her well. The vastness no longer frightens her. She now respects the water's dark depths, and the quick changes of weather and wind on the islands.

Nothing will ever be like it used to be. For a long time after she arrived in Sweden, she imagined they would soon be a family again. Mamma, Papa, Nellie, and Stephie. Now she knows that is never going to happen. Mamma is dead. Papa is gone, *abgereist*. And she is no longer a little girl.

Sixteen years old. Nearly grown up.

Her childhood is over.

She's already been in high school for a whole month. It's difficult, and she has to work hard, but she likes it. The girls are more serious than most of her classmates at grammar school were. They talk about current affairs and about what they want to be—teachers, pharmacists, or doctors, like Stephie. One of the girls even wants to be an engineer.

Every morning, Stephie and May take the tram to school. They bump into each other now and then in the halls, in the schoolyard, and in the lunchroom. After school they usually meet and take the tram back to Sandarna together.

A high wave tosses a cloud of foam up around her feet. Every seventh wave is an especially strong one, Stephie has heard. Why every seventh? She doesn't know.

Along another shore, farther south, the Allied troops are landing in France. A voice on the radio said, "This is not the beginning of the end, but it may be the end of the beginning." *How long is it going to take?*

Stephie sits down, pulling her knees to her chest and hugging them. She rests her chin on her hands. She becomes one with the rhythm of the waves, which helps her breathe more calmly.

At the far end of the beach, she sees a little figure approaching. After some time, Stephie recognizes Nellie. She's taken off her shoes and stockings and is wading barefoot in the shallow water, although it is already cold.

Stephie gets up and waves. "Nellie!" she shouts.

The wind carries her voice, and Nellie hears, looks up at the cliff, and waves back.

Stephie sits down again, waiting for Nellie to come along the beach. A stretch of shore is always longer than it appears. There are so many little coves to be walked around, rocks to be climbed over.

Shoes and socks in hand, Nellie heads up to where Stephie is sitting and drops down next to her. Silently, they look west, at the horizon, where the sea gleams bright silver. Closer to land, it still reflects the lead gray of the cloudy sky.

"We never made it to America," Nellie says after some time.

"No."

"You used to tell me about America. About big cities with tall buildings and streets crowded with cars. Do you remember?"

"Yes, I do."

"You comforted me," says Nellie. "When I was little."

Stephie looks at Nellie. Her face is grave and open.

"I've been angry with you," Nellie goes on. "I thought you were keeping me from feeling at home here. I thought you were always nagging, and giving me a guilty conscience."

"I had a guilty conscience myself, for failing to take

good enough care of you," Stephie says. "I felt like I was letting Mamma and Papa down."

They sit quietly, looking out over the endless sea. Stephie takes Nellie's hand, and Nellie doesn't pull away.

"We'll have to look after each other now," says Nellie.

"Yes," says Stephie. "We will."

ABOUT THE AUTHOR

ANNIKA THOR was born and raised in a Jewish family in Göteborg, Sweden. She has been a librarian, has written for both film and theater, and is the author of many books for children, young adults, and adults. She lives in Stockholm.

A Faraway Island, The Lily Pond, and *Deep Sea* are the first three novels in a quartet featuring the Steiner sisters, which has been translated into numerous languages and has garnered awards worldwide. Swedish television also adapted the books into a hugely popular eight-part series. *A Faraway Island* received the Mildred L. Batchelder Award for an outstanding children's book originally published in a foreign language, and *The Lily Pond* received the Mildred L. Batchelder Honor Award.